WHERE
THE LILIES
BLOOM

WHERE
THE LILIES
BLOOM

Vera and Bill Cleaver

HarperTrophy®
An Imprint of HarperCollinsPublishers

Where the Lilies Bloom
Copyright © 1969 by Vera and William J. Cleaver

Library of Congress Catalog Card Number 75-82402
ISBN 0-06-447005-9 (pbk.)

❖

First Harper Trophy edition, 1989

Visit us on the World Wide Web!
www.harperteen.com

To Jeanne Vestal

ONE

O NCE IN SOME NEAR-FORGOTTEN time a traveler, making his way across these mountains on foot, wandered into our valley which is known as Trial. Warm and dusty and overwearied, he came to our door and eased his heavy pack and asked for refreshment and Devola brought him a pail of water from our spring, pure and so cold it made him clench his teeth.

"Where have you been?" we asked.

He raised a khaki arm and pointed first to Sugar Boy that rises to our east and then to Old Joshua that lifts darkly to our west. "Up there."

"What for?"

"For the memory."

Devola thought this a funny answer. She laughed and ran down into the yard and hid herself behind a flowering rhododendron and

1

peered out at us through its white, lacy veil.

I said, "Don't pay her any mind. She's cloudy-headed. Why did you say you had been to Sugar Boy and Old Joshua for the memory? That wasn't a real answer, was it?"

"Yes," replied the traveler. "That was a real answer."

"They're pretty now," I said, "because everything is in bloom. Trillium and shadbush and the violets and all the other spring beauties but we've just come through a terrible winter. There was snow six feet deep in this valley with drifts up to ten. Everything was frozen; we thought it would never thaw. Romey and I couldn't even get to school."

"Who is Romey?" inquired the traveler.

"He's my little brother. In the winter when everything's frozen I hate the mountains. Then they're ugly."

The traveler said, "Today at noon I leaned my back against a cloud and ate my lunch. And afterward, coming down the slopes, I saw a lake of blue flowers and then a long, wide scarf of deep maroon ones. This is fair land; the fairest I have ever seen."

I never saw the traveler again. An hour later

he disappeared into the mists that sometimes cover this valley in the spring. But I have never forgotten what he said—that this land was fair land, the fairest of them all. This is where the lilies bloom.

Like I say, Devola is cloudy-headed and this is one thing I cannot understand because none of the rest of us Luthers is that way but Devola is for sure, so each day I have to explain the whole of our existence to her. Her confidence in my ability to do this is supreme though there are four whole years' difference between her age of eighteen and mine of fourteen.

Devola cannot remember twice around a gimlet. When we go, of a morning, to the lower slopes of Old Joshua or Sugar Boy to gather witch hazel leaves she always acts like she's never seen any of it before.

"Look!" she exclaims. "Look at how pretty it all is. Don't you think it's pretty, Mary Call?"

"Yes, it's pretty but we haven't got the time to stand around and gawk now, Devola. Oh, here we are. Here's where we left off yesterday. Aren't these leaves nice and thick? Shall we fill your bag first or mine?"

Devola shook her bag open and looked down into its emptiness. "It don't differ. Either way it's just plain work." She moved around to the north side of the witch hazel bush and began snatching the smooth, wavy-toothed leaves from its limbs. "How many pounds did we get yesterday?"

"Three. Don't put in twigs, Devola. Just leaves."

Devola fished two twigs out and discarded them. "How much is that?"

"Oh, forty-five cents, maybe."

"If that man at the drug company or Mr. Connell from the General Store had to come out here and do this for just one morning I'll bet it'd be a sight more than that. People are stingy with money, aren't they, Mary Call?"

"Some are."

A lance of clear sunlight wavering through the overhanging boughs touched Devola's face and hair. She stepped back away from it and turned and looked across the valley. In the distance Kiser Pease, high on his tractor, was creating clouds of furious, black dust. Between him and us the lonesome fields were a bright, shimmering yellow.

4

Devola said, "Kiser wants to marry me again but still Roy Luther says no. I told him it didn't differ to me one way or the other but that's all he says. No."

"You don't know anything about marriage, Devola. Aren't you going to help me pick any more?"

Devola came back to the bush. "Kiser's got a nice house. I just love his kitchen. Everything in it's yellow. Of course, he doesn't keep it good but I would. I'd wash everything every day."

"You would, huh?"

"Yes."

I referred to one of Kiser's superstitions, a keyhole opening he had made near the top of his chimney as an exit for witches. I asked, "Would you wash his witch's keyhole, too? Or would you plug it up so no more witches could get in or out?"

Devola smoothed her long cascade of glowing hair. "I wouldn't bother his keyhole. His witches wouldn't bother me. I just love his house. Just think; all of us could live in it if I married Kiser. You and Ima Dean and Romey and me and Roy Luther. All of us. Wouldn't that be nice?"

"No. We like it where we are. Devola, are you going to help me pick or aren't you?"

With a languishing look Devola picked two leaves. "Roy Luther owes Kiser money."

"Yeah, well he might get paid back someday."

Gently Devola deposited three twigs. "If Roy Luther was to give his say-so for me to marry Kiser, Kiser would forget about the money and give him twenty acres of land and the house we're living in."

"Roy Luther has already earned the land, Devola. Twenty times or more over. And he might just as well give us the house. It's falling down. Nobody else would have it."

"You don't like Kiser, do you, Mary Call?"

"No."

"Why?"

"Because he's ignorant. Nobody but an ignorant person would have a witch's keyhole in his house. And he's an old greedy gut and a cheat. There isn't another man in the whole world would come in here and sharecrop for him the way Roy Luther has for so little. Just years and years of it and when the time comes for tallying up, Kiser always getting the hog's share and Roy Luther always having to settle for the meanest."

6

Devola gazed at me. "I wish you wouldn't be so mad at everybody all the time. It makes you ugly. Kiser's lonesome," she offered. "He told me how lonesome he was."

"Yeah. Well, it's his own fault he hasn't got anybody. I've heard him brag about how he ran all his kin off years ago. This bush is stripped clean, Devola. Let's move on up a ways."

The August sun, full now in midmorning, was warm on our bare heads. Far above us Sugar Boy's spine loomed black-green. The air was richly peppered with the cool, sharp perfume of balsam and the soft, tepid scent of summer-fresh vegetation. Deep in a tangle of wild honeysuckle, a Carolina junco trilled his sweet bellsong.

Devola wears a look of suffering when she's made to come on these work-jaunts but it's like no other suffering I've ever seen. It's tender and sly and secret.

We located a new, fresh bush and I took one half and assigned the other half to Devola and obediently she moved around and began plucking, but in a minute parted the branches and looked at me through the wavy, green light. "Mary Call?"

"What?"

"I forgot my sack. I left it back yonder."

For Devola I have many fears and I have others, too. Some for our paternal parent, Roy Luther, and some for Ima Dean and Romey and a few for myself also. They are not rash. They are not just things that happened to fritter into my mind because nothing else was there to busy it. They are old fears with me.

Oh, I feel it, this bottomless stomach of fright when I look at Devola and see her so free and innocent, so womanly in form but with a child's heart and a child's mind. I feel it when I watch Ima Dean and Romey at their make-believe games. So carefree they are with never a thought in their little heads as to how they're going to get decently raised. And when I look at Roy Luther who is coughing his life away. (We know now that it isn't just worms that turn him so white and panting weak though we keep doctoring, laying out hope each time along with the salves and other medications.)

Roy Luther has made me promise him some things:

When the time comes, which he hopes will be in his sleep, I am to let him go on as quietly as he can, without any wailing and fussing. I am not to call any doctor or allow anyone else to call one. If it happens at night I am to wait until morning before I tell the others. I am not to send for the preacher or undertaker. The preacher has a mighty voice in these mountains but he expects to be paid for his wisdom. And the undertaker, for all his hushed, liquid speakings of how paltry his tariff will be, can be ill-humored and short-tempered when the time comes to divvy up as we found out in the case of Cosby Luther, my maternal parent, who died of the fever four years ago.

So it is that Roy Luther has requisitioned me to give him a simple, homemade burial when the time comes. After I am sure his heart and breathing have stopped, I am to wrap him in an old, clean sheet and take him to his final resting place which will be within a stand of black spruce up on Old Joshua. We have not talked about how I am to get him there. Were you to ask Roy Luther it would shame him to have to say aloud that it will have to be in Romey's wagon and he'd have to say what for me to do with the feet which will surely drag because the vehicle is but a toy.

I am worried about Roy Luther dying and how I am to get him decently and honorably buried but more than that I am worried about the other responsibilities he has charged me with, the other promises he has wrung from me.

Number one: I am always to take pride in having the name of Luther and instill this pride in the others, too. Number two: I am to strive with everything in me to keep our family together and not ever take charity from anybody even if our tongues hang out parched down to our knees because charity is seldom of real service to those upon whom it is bestowed and those who receive it are always looked upon with suspicion, every need and want scrutinized. Number three: I am to keep Devola with me always. I am to be good and kind and loving to her and see to it that the others are, too. I am not to let her marry Kiser Pease. If ever it looks to me like this is about to happen then I am to go to town, find the nearest judge, tell him about how Devola is, and get him to stop it.

On my word of highest honor I have promised Roy Luther all of these things. Just how I am to bring them about I don't know nor does he. Never a strong man or one able to think things out, he spends now most of his waking hours in his porch chair. The valley is there before him, big and rich and abundant but he doesn't see it anymore. The worms or whatever it is that started the sickness in him have taken all the caring out of him. Three or four times a day I ask him if he doesn't want me to doctor him and he always says yes and I fetch the bottle of turpentine and smear a good amount of the stuff around the base of his throat where he says the worms are the most active. It is a futile action and we both know it but when it's finished Roy Luther leans back and closes his eyes and says he feels better.

He's let things beat him, Roy Luther has. The land, Kiser Pease, the poverty. Now he's old and sick and ready to die and when he does, this is what we'll inherit—his defeat and all that goes with it.

Sometimes when I look at him I am stirred to an unholy anger. I think, God help me, Roy Luther, I don't want you dead and that's the truth. But since it's going to happen anyhow I wish it could hurry up and be over with for it's pulling us all to pieces and I need to get on with things and try to fix them around so that life will be easier for those of us who are left.

And I get scared and I think, but how am I going to do this? Who will show me how and who will help me?

And then I get madder and I say to myself, Aw, quit your bellyaching. There's a way; all you have to do is find it.

Oh, that witch hazel leaves weighed a pound apiece. Going home I expressed this wry wish to Devola but she just smiled and said she was hungry.

We are mountain people so we eat mountain food. Liver mush and fried cabbage and cranberry beans cooked to nutty goodness with slabs of thick fatback. Devola is good about the cooking and Ima Dean and Romey are good about eating what's set before them. They don't whine when I tell them that there's nothing to sweeten the end of a plain meal. Ima Dean just softly draws in her breath and says, "Well, maybe tomorrow." And with a manly look Romey says, "I wasn't even thinkin' about anything sweet. I was thinkin' about the mountains, how old they are. Do you know, Mary Call?"

How old are the Great Smoky Mountains? A

hundred years? Two? Why can't I have some books so I can find out the answers to a few things? So I wouldn't have to stand here shamed in front of this child and admit to him that I don't know how old the Great Smoky Mountains are?

Romey is looking at me. He says, "It's all right, Mary Call. Don't fret yourself about it. I'll find out, sometime."

It's not all right with me not to know this. I need to correct my ignorance. I need so many things.

TWO

I N THE EVENING OF THE DAY OF WHICH I
write about now Roy Luther had an attack
that left him queer in his thinking.

Just at dusk he rose from his chair on the
porch and started out across to the steps but
never reached them. He stopped suddenly and
put one hand up to the back of his neck and a
vague look wrinkled his brow. He took one step
more and then something unseen savagely tore
into him. Across his face there swept rigid sur-
prise and then bursting agony and then his
scream rang out, profaning the stillness. He
pitched forward.

Devola came running and we got him into
the house and up in his bed. Crumpled there, he
held his temples desperately with both hands
and was wretchedly sick. We cleaned the vomit
and applied cold cloths and covered him with a

cotton blanket. We didn't say the word doctor. Roy Luther doesn't hold with doctors. In his opinion all that doctors knew how to do is cut. One had killed his mother, slicing into the ugly, shriveled growth on her neck, letting in the contaminated air. No doctor had ever stepped foot inside Roy Luther's house and none ever would. Home medicine was a sight better than any doctor could bring.

Devola made Roy Luther tamarack tea which he couldn't keep down at first but after the first long night had come and gone some of the hot, resin-scented liquid stayed in his stomach. I made poultices of gum camphor and turpentine and laid one on the back of his neck and the other on his stomach. I was struck by the fact that now his eyes were no longer alike. The pupil in the right one was much larger than that in the left. His right eye now seemed to be permanently fixed higher in his face. He couldn't speak though Ima Dean and Romey sat beside his bed for hours at a time and in fearful whispers begged him to. To me it seemed like Roy Luther only had a handful of days left and I prayed that the end would come in the night because if it came in the day I would have my hands too full with trying to explain to Romey and Ima Dean what had happened. I'd have to lock them out of the room where Roy Luther lay and I wouldn't dare to let them see how bad I felt myself because if I did any carrying on they'd cut loose, too. My mind kept shuttling backward and forward and over and around this worry and all the others, too, and there weren't any answers anywhere.

This time—some four or five days of it—was foreverness. Each morning I went alone for the witch hazel leaves. Devola stayed behind and cared for Roy Luther and the house. Ima Dean cut herself a whole new doll family from the Sears catalogue and stuffed the paper figures in fruit jars where they curled; Roy Luther lay on his bed in the cool, darkened room scarcely breathing. Romey said it looked to him like now he was the man of the family and put on his old boots and struck out across the fields, hoisting his hoe like a banner. That twisted my heart because Romey is just barely ten years old and has none of the rough makings of a farm boy.

On about the sixth day Devola reported to me that Roy Luther was some better, that he had been able to eat a little.

"What did he eat?" I asked.

She said, "Some beans and cornbread. And he drank a little tea with sugar in it. I held him up."

I went in and looked at Roy Luther. He's shrinking, I thought. When we brought him in here his bed was almost too small for him but now he's lost in it. He's shrinking and maybe this will just keep on until there's nothing of him left.

I said, "Roy Luther?"

He opened his eyes and focused the good one on me and tried to speak but couldn't. Just a thick, foamy sound came out.

Toward sundown Romey came in from the fields with the suggestion that there might be something wrong with Kiser Pease. I asked him what made him think so and he said, "Well, I haven't seen any smoke from his chimney for two days and I haven't seen him either. The last time I did he was coughing pretty bad. Said he was sick in the chest."

I said, "He's sick in the head, that's where he's sick." And everybody laughed and Romey washed up and Devola dished supper and in a lighter mood we sat down and ate.

Romey said he knew where there was a big

spread of lamb's-quarters which is a potherb, something like spinach. He said he had spotted it that morning. So after supper he and I took a basket and some knives and lit out for Trial Creek which runs through the furthermost back section of Kiser's land.

In the evening gloam Old Joshua and Sugar Boy loomed big against the facing sky, and their foothills shadowed in blue gloom. The wind, sweeping down the valley, was fresh and brisk and I said to Romey that I smelled rain coming and that maybe we'd get caught in it.

He looked up and calculated and said, "No. By the time it gets here we'll be close to Kiser's house and can take shelter on his porch or in his garage. Come on, let's run."

For all of his being so slight and fine-boned Romey has amazing strength and can run faster than anything with two legs I ever saw. He beat me to the lamb's-quarters bed by ten lengths.

The light was waning and now the summer rain was closer, hovering thick over the mountaintops. On the opposite side of the creek something among the black-shadowed hardwoods crashed.

Kneeling beside me, Romey gave pure

attention to the tender green shoots. He said, "Wouldn't it be funny if that was a bear over there? What would you do if it was, Mary Call?"

I said, "I'd sprout wings and fly out of here faster'n any airplane ever built. It'd only take me about two minutes to get to Asheville."

On his haunches Romey moved around so that he was between me and the wind. He said, "Tomorrow I'm going to bring Roy Luther's gun down here and see if maybe I can't bag us some squirrels. Fried squirrel goes good with this stuff. What're you thinkin' about, Mary Call?"

"Nothing."

"About Roy Luther?"

"Maybe."

"He's going to leave us, isn't he?"

"He might."

Romey's eyes and mouth, pale in the dusky light, were gravely steady. "If he does, what will we do?"

"I don't know. I've been trying to think ahead but I haven't figured it out yet."

"Kiser'll make us move."

"Maybe."

"If he does, where will we go?"

"I don't know. Somewhere. We're going to live, Romey. Don't worry about things."

Romey turned his head and looked at me. "He's too old for Devola, isn't he, Mary Call?"

"Yes. Kiser's most forty and Devola's only eighteen."

A drop of rain fell on Romey's cheek and then another and far away lightning bolted and thunder sounded and we looked up and saw the rain moving down the valley toward us in great, wavering sheets and Romey said we'd best not be caught out in the open. I tied the dishcloth I'd brought along tight over the mouth of the basket so that none of the greens would spill out and we rose and ran back along the bank to Kiser's house.

All of the front windows were wide open and so was the door but there wasn't a light on anywhere. And there weren't any sounds at all.

Romey tried the screen door and said, "It's not latched. You reckon it'd be all right if we just went in?"

"Wait." I said. And walked back to the edge of the porch and peered out through the darkness. Kiser's car was in the garage, the back end of it gleaming whitely. "He's here," I said. "But there's

20

something wrong. As stingy as he is he wouldn't leave all the windows open like this, wouldn't take a chance on the rain ruining his curtains and floors. Let's just step inside a minute, Romey."

Romey went in ahead of me and located the electric switch just inside and pressed it. "Look," he said. And I looked and there was Kiser Pease sprawled on the davenport. One of his boots had soiled the fine green upholstery; there was a stubble of beard on his face and dried spittle around his mouth. His eyes were wide open but delirium-glazed. From his knees to his chin he had swathed himself in three heavy, woolen blankets but still in this odd half-sleep of his, his teeth chattered.

Romey said, "Lord have mercy, look at him. He's sicker'n a dog. He don't even know we're here, he's that sick. Wonder how long he's been this way."

I said, "Close the windows and the door, Romey. And draw the curtains. It's terribly damp and cold in here. What does he do for heat in this place or is he too stingy to have any?"

Romey said no, that Kiser had heat and clattered down the basement steps and fired up the furnace there and in just a few minutes warmth began to seep into the room. There was a bowl of cold, untouched soup on the table beside the davenport. I carried it to the kitchen and dumped it down the sink. Through all of our activities Kiser didn't stir. There was just the sound of his teeth chattering and his ragged breathing. Romey moved a footstool and chair over and we sat down in front of Kiser and looked at him and wondered aloud to each other what was to be done.

Romey said, "Maybe a snake bit him and he's still got the fangs in him. You think we oughta look, Mary Call?"

"No."

"What then?"

"Hush a minute. I'm thinking."

Prissy, like a girl, Romey folded his hands in his lap and closed his eyes. The rain breathed against the sides of the house. I thought about hot chocolate and how fragile life is and how much of everything it takes to sustain it.

Kiser whimpered suddenly and pulled at the blankets. His eyelids drooped and two skimpy tears rolled down. He can't even cry generous, I thought, and leaned forward and felt the heat coming from him. His breath and the sight of his stained teeth, with dark brown pockets along the gum lines, recoiled me. None of us Luthers has ever had a bought toothbrush. We make our own from white birch branches and we make our own cleaner from wintergreen leaves and table salt but all of us have strong, white teeth and red gums, even Ima Dean who is only five.

Romey had opened his eyes and was staring at Kiser. The edges of his face were very sharp. He moved his feet back and forth on the rung of his chair. "He's real sick, ain't he?"

"Isn't he, Romey. Isn't he. Don't say ain't."

"Well, isn't he, then. He's real sick, isn't he?"

"Yes."

"He doesn't even know we're here, does he?"

"No, I don't think so."

"He can't hear what we're saying, can he?"

"No."

Romey's smile was wide and angelic. He stilled his feet and rested his dirty hands on his knees. In a tone of hushed, near-reverence he said, "Kiser's whole basement is full of food, Mary Call."

"Is it? What kind?"

"All kind. There must be near to two dozen

hams hanging from the rafters down there. And he's got a freezer full of butter and chicken and all kinds of stuff. Those hams were real hickory-cured. Boy, they look good. What you reckon he's going to do with all of them?"

"I don't know, Romey."

"He's breathing kind of funny. He's breathing just like Grandpa Luther did when he was dying. Maybe he's got pneumonia like Grandpa and fixin' to die. Are we going to do anything for him?"

"In a minute we might. I'm still thinking."

"About what?"

Kiser's tongue was out of his mouth. The tip of it searched in vain for moisture. A pulse in his neck fluttered. He looked helpless and somehow strangely sincere.

He'll do it, I thought. He's got no choice but to do it. I'll tell him he's got to. I'll pull him out of this just far enough so's he'll be able to understand what I'm talking about and then I'll tell him.

Romey was looking at me, not sighing but ready to. He found a patch of dried soil on his knee and rubbed it with his palm. His sigh came. He said, "Well, if you don't want to tell me I don't care. It's too hot in here now and I'm tired. If we aren't going to do anything about him let's go home. The rain's stopped."

I said, "Romey, we're going to help Kiser. We aren't going to let him die. If he died he wouldn't be any good to us. You understand?"

"No, Mary Call."

"We need onions. Lots of onions. You remember seeing any down in the basement?"

"No. I wasn't looking for onions. I was looking at the hams."

Romey's hunger for things we don't have never leaves him.

We went down to the basement and found onions, bushels of them, heaped white and red and yellow in ventilated bins along the wall.

I said, "We'll need a basket or something so we can get them upstairs."

Remembrance surged into Romey's face. He groaned. "Oh, no, not *that* treatment." But he helped me fill an old galvanized washtub with onions and between us we got it up to the kitchen.

Romey said were we going to doctor Kiser where he was or were we going to transfer him to the bathroom and were we going to do it with his underwear on or off, and that Ima Dean and Devola would be worried about us and shouldn't he run home and tell them what was going on.

I said we'd give Kiser his treatment in the bathroom and we'd leave his underwear on, and for Romey to run home and tell Ima Dean and Devola what was going on and bring them back with him. Roy Luther would sleep the night through without waking.

While Romey was gone I started peeling the onions, slicing them and frying them. In two deep, cast-iron pots with the heat under them turned low so they wouldn't burn, they sizzled and steamed and the house filled with the smell of them and rich, hot peanut oil.

I went in once for a look at Kiser to make sure he was still alive. He thought I was his sister.

"Sister, I'm a-dyin', Sister. Oh, I knowed you'd come. I knowed it. Bygones is bygones now. Oh, I knowed I packed a lot of things off on to you that wasn't right but I'm a-repentin' for 'em now. You say it, Sister. Bygones is bygones. You say it. Bygones is bygones."

To try and quiet him I said, "Bygones is bygones."

He pushed himself up and clutched my arm. "Oh, I see them devil eyes a-shinin' and I hear them devil voices a-screechin'. Make 'em stop, Sister! I don't want to go nowhars with them! O Lordy, I'm a-dyin' and I don't deserve to. I never did nothin' wrong to nobody."

I said, "You never did anything right to anybody, Kiser, and you do so deserve to die but I'm not going to let you. You want a drink of water?"

He let me hold the glass to his mouth and some of the water went down him but most of it spilled because his teeth were chattering so.

Romey came back with Ima Dean and Devola. Devola looked at Kiser and said he looked sick and looked at the kitchen and said what a mess and I said, "Never mind that now. Just you and Ima Dean start peeling and frying. But first help Romey and me get Kiser into the bathroom."

He moaned when we first tried to move him and nobody sympathized. "It's not our fault you're so fat," said Romey. "You oughta try going hungry once in a while."

"He'd be lighter," Ima Dean pointed out, "if his boots were off." So we tried to remove them but couldn't. He had stuffed his long underwear, which he wears summer and winter, down into his boots and his feet were wedged in tight.

"He smells," complained Devola. "We should give him a bath before we do whatever we're fixin' to do with him."

Romey said, "If you was to ask me this dirty old bird ain't worth saving from nothing, least of all death, but if we're going to do it, let's do it." And he grasped Kiser under one arm and Devola took him by the other and I took his right leg and Ima Dean took his left one and we staggered to the bathroom with him and deposited him in the cold tub. He started to shake violently but not for long. I had Romey bring all the blankets he could find and we slipped these under Kiser and tucked them all around him good and tight and then Devola brought in the first kettle of fried onions and Romey and I started the treatment. We opened up Kiser's underwear to the waist and slathered him thick with the hot onions front and back and then Devola brought another kettleful and I steamed a towel under the hot water tap and poured the second batch into it, making Kiser a collar and then Ima Dean said what about his head and I hollered for Devola to bring more onions and made Kiser a cap from another towel and more onions.

The bathroom was small and hot and steamy and Kiser, writhing and pitching in his nest of blankets and warm, oily onions, began to pant and sweat.

I sat on the side of the tub and Romey closed the toilet seat and sat on it and we watched.

Kiser didn't like being all plastered up with the onions. Devola brought in another potful and we dumped that down inside his underwear and he gagged and sputtered and slid around and tried to climb out of the tub but Romey and I pushed him back down and wrapped the blankets tighter around him.

"I've smelled some stenches," observed Romey. "But I do believe this here one is the worst. Look, Mary Call. His cap has slipped off. Maybe you'd better tie the towel under his chin. No, wait a minute. I'll go see if I can find some big safety pins. They'll work better than tying. And I'll have Devola bring some fresh onions. These here on his head are all turned cold."

Relieved of his cap Kiser worked his arm free of the blankets and clawed onions out of his hair and ears and coughed and gasped and wheezed.

I leaned over him and said, "Kiser? It's Mary Call Luther. Do you recognize me?"

Under its burden of onions and blankets Kiser's chest rose and fell. His tongue came out and licked his lips. His colorless eyes, staring into mine, were filled with bewilderment. "Sister?" he croaked. "Sister? Oh, Sister, I'm a-dyin'. Ain't no use to beg the truth with me now. I'm a-dyin'."

It was still too early to try any reasoning with him.

Slippery with onions herself all up and down her front, Devola came in with a steaming black brew of coltsfoot and turpentine and spicewood all boiled up together and we got a cupful down him. Devola said Romey was fixing us a little night supper to eat and was one ham enough to slice and fry?

Along about midnight Kiser was able to talk some sense to me. Romey's fried ham and Devola's biscuits, slathered thick with real butter and sourwood honey, had sustained us that long.

Still in his nest of onions, some of them warmed over, and oily blankets, Kiser's skin suddenly changed hue. Some of the fever in it ebbed and it took on a papery look.

Curled on the toilet seat, Romey said, "Something's happening to him, Mary Call. Look."

Kiser had come partly awake, was hovering in that queer ambience between consciousness and unconsciousness with his exhausted eyes on me, trying to place me, and his drained mouth groping for sound. It came out of his throat in chopped little halts. "Mary Call . . . is . . . that . . . you?"

"Yes, Kiser."

"What? Wha's trouble?"

"You're sick, Kiser. Awful sick. I'm helping you. Devola and I. We've been here since day before yesterday. When we found you, you were dying. You still might be. We'll know by maybe . . . oh, tomorrow morning. No, don't try to move, Kiser. What you've got to do now is just lie there quiet as you can and try to recover. Devola and I are right here helping you. See?"

Weakly Kiser's eyes slid around to Romey. "Devola . . . she looks different," he whispered.

"Yeah. Well, you'd look different, too, if you had been here two nights and two days fighting the pneumonia and fever in you the way we

31

have. We almost gave you up for a goner a couple of times, Kiser, and that's the truth. You were very sick. You still are. Isn't that right, Devola?"

Romey nodded.

Against impending tragedy Kiser closed his eyes. A pale, translucent piece of exhausted onion slid out from beneath his turban and slowly traveled down the bridge of his nose. He didn't brush it away.

"Kiser?"

"Wha'?"

"You're very sick."

"Wuuuuuuuuh. Sick."

"If Devola and I went away and left you now you'd die. You hear me, Kiser?"

"Wuuuuuuuuh. I'd die."

"We don't want to go away and leave you."

"No, don't leave me."

"But the thing is I can't think of any good reason why we should stay. Not one."

In a swift, little tide the fever returned to Kiser's cheeks. Another onion slid down, this time on his eyelid. He tried to blink it off but it stuck. His breath started to come hard and fast. "I'd . . . pay you."

"With what, Kiser?"

"Wuuuuuuuuh, money."

"How much?"

". . . Five dollars, mebbe."

"I don't want five dollars, Kiser."

". . . Don't want five dollars?"

"No."

"Wuuuuuuuuh. Don't leave me. . . . Sick. Terrible sick."

"I want you to give us the house we live in and the land Roy Luther works. Free and clear. I want you to sign a paper that says so."

". . . Wha' paper?"

"This paper."

Kiser signed the paper. I waved the ink dry, folded it and tucked it under the inner lining of my shoe.

"What does it mean?" asked Romey.

"It means we're free," I said. "Now we own our own house and our own land. There's twenty acres of it and nobody can even set foot on it unless we want them to. Not even Kiser. We're not farm tenants anymore, Romey. Now nobody can tell us what to do. We're free."

Romey stood and took three steps and looked down at Kiser. Kiser had his eyes closed, was breathing evenly. His towel turban had slipped sideways allowing pieces of lank hair and strings of wearied onion to escape. He was dirty and greasy and gaunt. He looked terrible—worse than I'd ever seen him. But still, in that time, in that moment, I saw in him something I'd never seen before. It might have been just a feeling or it might have been real but I saw it—a curious, raw dignity. And I thought, He's mean and he's stingy and he's a bully and he's gone back on his word to Roy Luther more times than anybody can count but he won't go back on this. I won't let him. He'll try it and I'll have to fight him and maybe I won't be any match for him but I won't go down the way Roy Luther's gone. I won't let him do to me and the rest who belong to me what he's done to Roy Luther.

Romey was saying, "You mean from now on when I'm out in the fields working and Kiser comes riding up and hollers for me to do something I don't have to do it?"

"That's right. That's exactly what I mean."

"He might go back on what the paper says, Mary Call. He might just go back on it."

I said, "No, he won't. I won't let him."

For our night's work Romey figured we

should have a little something extra. I argued that we couldn't take anything; that if we did it would be stealing. He found a piece of paper and a pencil and wrote out an IOU to Kiser. He didn't put any amount on it, just listed the things we took from the basement: a ham, four frozen chickens, four pounds of frozen butter, two quarts of honey, a peck of red yams. Romey found a gunnysack for the yams and let Ima Dean drag them home. They were too heavy for her to carry.

THREE

ROY LUTHER TOOK HIS SHARE OF THE
chicken in soup. Devola made it rich
with homemade egg noodles floating
around on its glistening top and Roy Luther
seemed to enjoy it. He let me spoon it to him
three times a day and after each feeding would
try to smile his gratitude and I said to Devola
and the others that I thought he was gradually
getting better. Devola sponge-bathed him daily
and changed his nightshirt and bed clothing. The
hair on his head grew long and she took the
home barber clippers and gave him a round,
feminine haircut and the black hair on his face
flourished, and she took his razor to it but complained that the blade scraped and said when I
took my witch hazel leaves to Connell's General
Store could I please get her a new one if it didn't
cost too much.

I said yes but kept putting off making the trip. It was a long walk to the General Store—five miles to it and five miles from it. Such a walk consumes shoe leather so it shouldn't be done any more often than was absolutely necessary. Besides I was waiting for Kiser Pease to come. Most a week had passed now since we had saved him from dying and I was anxious to get things out into the open between us so that we could get matters settled firm and sure.

Morose and impatient, Romey suggested that maybe Kiser had, after all, just gone on and died but in the same breath reported smoke rising from Kiser's chimney.

Something had flown out of Romey. Now he couldn't be light and careless about things but had to know reasons and be furnished explanations. He wanted to know how much this cost and that and this and that and where was the money for it all coming from. The Luther money had always been kept in a tin box on a kitchen shelf and he took it down and counted it again and again but couldn't make it more than the fifty-four dollars and eighty-four cents that it was.

"It isn't going to grow," I said, "until we make it."

He glared at me. "How're we going to make it?"

"I don't know yet. Don't worry about it."

"You keep saying that but *you're* worried."

"No I'm not. I'm just thinking."

"About what?"

"Things."

"What things?"

"Just things. I've got an idea but it's hiding. I just have to give it time to come out and be recognized."

"If you had an idea," said Romey with somber logic, "you wouldn't have to wait for it to come out and be recognized. You'd have it right there in your brain. Tell me about the land again."

"The land is ours now, Romey. All twenty acres of it."

"We going to work it?"

"Sure. Come spring we will."

"What with? If we're our own people now and can't look to Kiser Pease anymore, not for anything, we won't be able to ask him for the use of his horses or his tractor or anything. What'll we plant?"

"What we've always planted."

"Cabbage?"

"Sure."

"And potatoes?"

"Yes."

"How will we get them to market?"

"I don't know. I haven't figured that part out yet."

"Looks to me," said Romey, "like we need to figure out a lot of things. With winter coming on soon the land isn't good for anything except to just lay out there and rest. Except for Roy Luther's little patch of truck garden and a few hills of potatoes, Kiser's picked it clean for this year. Our part of it anyway. Kiser's still got corn and stuff on his but if you noticed, our part has been picked barer than a bird's behind."

It was true. Except for an occasional dejected stalk, a few forgotten potatoes, and Roy Luther's plot of vegetable garden the Luther land had been plucked clean. Now it would lie fallow until spring.

But in the meantime there was this other— this little knot of an idea tucked away in some forgotten pigeon-hole-of-mind. Resting there, just waiting for whatever it would take to prod it back to useful life.

I know when this happened. It happened during the blackest part of one night when a turbulence of thick mist rose up out of the bowels of Old Joshua and made watery trails across the face of the moon. My bed suddenly turned cold and I left it and went to the window and looked out and thought I saw something—a figure kneeling in a blur of white haze on the dark grass. I thought it was Devola and called out to her and just when I did it all dissolved and I moved back from the window and stood there for a minute, feeling the rise of a slow excitement. And then I went across the hall to the room where Roy Luther slept and tiptoed in past him to the chest that had been my mother's, and removed the afghan that she had knitted in the last year of her life from its top and opened its lid and dug down and found it—a big, thick volume that had belonged to Cosby Luther named *A Guide to Wildcrafting*.

And with the excitement in me beating hard I carried the book to the cold kitchen and built a fire in the wood stove and sat beside it until the night was gone and read about ginseng and mayapple and goldenseal and all the rest of the medicine plants that grow wild in the green forests of Appalachia—plants which drug companies the world over gladly pay for.

"Wild Gold," I said aloud and the fire in the stove crackled afresh and in the slowly lightening yard Ima Dean's pet bantam rooster crowed.

Kiser came that morning—came riding across the sun-drenched fields on his big chestnut roan. When he got to our front gate he reined in and hollered for Roy Luther to come out and Romey started from his breakfast chair but I waved him back—went out and confronted Kiser by myself.

His sickness hadn't improved Kiser's looks any. It had thinned him so that his clothes hung limp and his skin hung haggard. His yellowed eyes were lackluster and his mouth was wrinkled.

His roan was pawing the earth, his hoofs sending up little geysers of black dust and I said to Kiser to kindly move him out of my flower bed, couldn't he see he was sitting smack in the middle of it?

Kiser pulled at the reins and the roan moved backward.

Kiser said, "Where's ye daddy, Mary Call?"

"He's sick in bed and it won't do you any good to holler for him because he can't move and he can't talk. I'm glad you rode over, Kiser. There's a little something I need to talk over with you."

Kiser passed the back of one hand over his mouth, studied me for a second, slid down from the roan. Tolerant and amused he said, "Mary Call, I pity the man you'uns marry. Do you know I ain't ever seen you when you *didn't* have somethin' to talk to me about? You understand now that it don't pain me none. Most times I enjoy it but this morning I just shore can't spare the time. I come to talk to Roy Luther."

I let him go by himself. While he was gone I took a stick and repaired as best I could the damage the roan had done to my primroses planted in thick rows all along the outside fence. The crystalline air was sharp and cool in my lungs.

Romey came out and said that Kiser was in the room with Roy Luther and should he go back and listen at the door. I reminded him that the Luthers were not door-crack listeners and sent him out to Roy Luther's garden to pick the last of the sweet corn and tomatoes. He protested some but he went.

Kiser was with Roy Luther about twenty minutes. That the visit shook him up some was written all over him plain as day when he came back out to me. With steps weighted slow and expression weighted heavy he came and put his hands on the top rail of the gate and looked down at me and with a queer kind of sorrow in his ugly face said, "Wal."

"You see how it is," I said.

Kiser pushed the gate open and came outside and leaned down and took the stick out of my hands. "I thought you wanted them fleurs to live," he said. "But you're a-killin' 'em."

I stood up and faced him then, eye to eye. "So you see how it is with us now."

Kiser tossed the stick away. He sucked his teeth and ran his tongue around his dry, cracked lips. "Wal," he said, "he's in a bad way sure. I seen his kind of sickness before. Hit'll worsen, is about the only thing can be said for it."

"It might," I said. "But maybe not. If I had my way I'd have him to a doctor but he'd never stand still for it. It'd just kill him quicker."

Kiser hooked a thumb inside his belt. He turned his head, tilting it so that his hat fell back a little, and studied Sugar Boy like he'd never seen it before. He said, "Wal, I wisht I knew how to advise you'uns, Mary Call. I sure wisht I did but I don't. If it'd be any help to you, you could stay on here awhile. Least-aways till spring. I wouldn't charge you nothin'. But just havin' a roof over your heads ain't goin' to settle everythin', you know. I don't suppose Roy Luther's got any money saved?"

I said, "No, he hasn't got any money saved."

Kiser took his hat off and scratched his head. "Wal," he said. "That's too bad. A fella always should lay by a little bit for a rainy day. I sure wisht I knew how to advise you, Mary Call. I sure do but I don't. The only thing I can think of is maybe the county people in town would help you. Give you enough to live on until somethin' else turns up. Yeah, you could do that. I know a fella over in Pumpkin Holler gets ninety dollars a month from the county people. Told me it wasn't much of a job to talk 'em into doin' it. If I'd be you I'd study it over, Mary Call. You know, you're a-gonna have to have some help from somebody."

I looked out across the ravaged fields and saw Romey, a vaporous figure in the distance, moving around in Roy Luther's garden. He had a gunnysack slung over one shoulder and the bottom of this bulged but not much.

A few ears of corn and a few tomatoes and that'll be it, I thought. And then I thought: That's been Roy Luther's whole life. A few tomatoes and a few ears of corn grown on somebody else's land from seed paid for by somebody else. And for every scrap always having to toady and apologize. Always having to say yes, Kiser, and no, Kiser, and thank you, Kiser, and I'm sorry, Kiser. For what?

What had we been thanking him for all this time? You don't thank people who set you in bondage and hold you there year after wretched year. You hate them. And if it isn't in you to hate, as it never had been in Roy Luther, then you do second best; you pick up and get out. And if that isn't possible you start making plans to make it so. Do something. Do anything. But don't just stand there and let people beat on you and then thank them for doing it.

Kiser who had left off studying Sugar Boy and had moved on out to stand beside the roan was saying, "Wal, I bist be gettin' on. You let me know what you aim to do, Mary Call. Like I say, you could stay on here till spring if you was a mind. I wouldn't charge you nothin'. That way you'd have a roof over your head for the winter. I'd be a-losin' money. This house'd bring a good rent if I was a mind to let it out to somebody else but Roy Luther and me has been friends for a long time. I'd be a mighty pore stick if I didn't do what I could for him now."

Something inside me began to work. I could feel its cold, slow spread pushing up to crowd my ribs and my heart and my lungs. Devola and Ima Dean had come to the front door and were anxiously, silently looking out at us and Kiser turned his head and looked at Devola. In the distant garden Romey shifted the gunnysack from one shoulder to the other. He's too thin, I thought. All of them are. They deserve something better than what they're getting but there's no one now except me to even try to get it for them and I don't know how and I'm scared but here goes.

I said, "Kiser, I can tell you right now what I aim to do. I've known since the night Devola and I and Romey and Ima Dean saved you from dying what I aimed to do. I aim for me and my family to stay on here in this house you gave us and come spring we'll work the land you gave us and we'll be our own people now and not look to you for anything and don't you look to us for anything either and that's the way it's going to be."

Kiser's interest in Devola fled. He blinked and jerked around to me. "What, Mary Call? What's this? *I* gave you this house? *I* gave you this land? Who says so?"

"You signed a paper, Kiser. The night you were dying you did. It was a bargain between us. You said if we saved you from dying you'd give us the house and the land around it—twenty acres of it—and I agreed to it and wrote it out and you signed it. You want to see the paper?"

"Yes," answered Kiser and watched me kneel again and take the paper from my shoe.

"If I let you hold it while you read it," I said, "can I have your word that you won't tear it up?"

Kiser's eyes had filled with a still, glittered expression. It acknowledged who I was—my stature in this business we were transacting. So strangely it did this, as if each of us, in that moment, had suddenly been converted into having a respect for each other. It wasn't true of course. I had no more respect for Kiser Pease than I had for a clod of dirt and his for me could be measured about the same. But just in that moment, for some reason not explainable, there was an unspoken exchange of respect and trust.

"Let me see the paper," said Kiser, without promising not to tear it up and I handed it to him.

FOUR

I GATHERED THEM, MY FAMILY, AROUND ME and told them about the big change that had taken place in our lives. It's certain now, I said. Oh, I wish you could have been out there with me. It was the funniest thing. Kiser just read the paper, handed it back to me, climbed up on his roan and rode off. He didn't say more than twenty words.

"What words did he say?" asked Romey.

"He wished us luck."

"Is that all?"

"No. And then he said the price of freedom comes mighty dear sometimes."

"What freedom?"

"Romey, I don't know. Any freedom. I suppose he was talking about any freedom. All freedom. He didn't know what he was talking about. He just said that."

"He was looking at me," murmured Devola. "I saw him. He still wants to marry me. Oh, his house is so big and nice. If Roy Luther was to let me marry Kiser we all could live in his house. He has hot water all the time. I just love hot water."

Ima Dean thrust her hand inside one of her fruit jars, withdrew two paper dolls and carefully tore their heads off.

Romey laid his hand on my arm and leaned to look deep into my eyes. "So now we're free but what does it mean? I still don't know what it means we're supposed to do. Have you thought of your idea yet?"

"Yes," I answered and brought out the plant book and instructed them to gather around and we studied it.

Ima Dean said that the foxglove plant with its delicately flared blossoms, varying in color from white to deep rose and purple, was rightly named; that one time while she was out in the forest alone, she had seen a red fox prancing around with a pair of them on.

Devola said what's digitalis and Romey grabbed the book around and said, "We just read what it was. It's the drug they get from foxglove.

Can't you remember anything, Devola? We're done with foxglove. Now we're on ginseng. You see the picture of this plant? This is ginseng. Now when we go out looking for plants this is what we should look for the hardest because it brings the most money. It grows in the shade, mostly under hickory and beech and maple trees. A good root of this comes out of the ground in the shape of a man."

"What man?" inquired Devola.

"Any man," answered Romey and began reading aloud to us about what it was used for—in face creams and tonics and as a cure for numerous ailments. We learned about mayapple which yields the powerful drug podophyllin, lobelia herb from which is made a medicinal tincture used in the treatment of asthma and bronchitis. We learned about queen's-delight and star grass root and all the rest of the paying plants.

"We'll be rich," said Ima Dean and went on to describe what she'd buy with her share of the money earned—a car like Kiser's with a squirrel tail flying from its hood.

Devola said she'd like a yellow dress with shoes to match.

Speculating, Romey closed the book and laid it aside. "If this here's such a good idea how come Roy Luther never did any wildcraftin'?"

I said I didn't know but I think I did. Roy Luther's pride, I think, had stood in the way of his doing any of it. It would be his notion that twigs and leaves and roots are child's play. A man should toil in the fields.

Romey said, "Well, let's get started. What are we waiting for? Aren't we going to start today?"

I said, "No. Tomorrow. Today I need to go to the General Store and talk to Mr. Connell. You can go with me. We'll take the witch hazel leaves and get our money for those."

Romey is a good walking companion. He doesn't chatter like Ima Dean or run ahead and every which way like Devola.

Under the cope of the blue sky Trial Valley lay in a quietus in the midmorning sun. It was awash with clear green and yellow light. High above a distant ridge two red-tailed buzzards lazily wheeled. The wind was idle and careless and faintly scented.

Burdened down with his divided share of the witch hazel leaves, Romey sniffed the wind and said how good it smelled and what made it and

I said, you know what makes it. It's the earth and the trees and the flowers. Everything all put together makes it. This is fair land. Probably the fairest in all of this whole country. You'll soon find out how fair it is. You've never really looked before but now you're going to. All of us are. This land is going to be good to us. You'll see.

Romey laughed and sniffed the air again and I sniffed it too and thought about freedom—the wondrous glory in it and its awful anxiety—and we walked on.

I have known Mr. Connell from the time I was four—him and his General Store so wonderfully cluttered with the shoes right next to the meat counter, some of them spilled out of their white tissue paper and boxes. The United States Post Office was in one front corner, hiding behind a rack of olive-drab raincoats and long tables of grab-bag pots and pans. A bouquet of brooms, tied together with a cord of stout twine, leaned against a butcher's block on which there rested a huge round of yellow rat cheese draped over with a length of brown, oiled paper. There were cans of pineapple on the school supply shelf and a row of flyspecked jars with the candies inside them stuck together; and over and through all this and more was the smell of leather and dry goods and country ham and dried wintergreen and dust that's so old it's lost its color and life.

Mr. Connell himself is the color of dust. He is short and meaty and melancholy. His wife is tall and stringy and has a dishonest smile. She does not like us Luthers. Sitting straight as a ramrod in her rocker, with her hands idle and her gaunt mouth plastered thin and pale, she elicits information:

"I hear your daddy's on the go-down, Mary Call."

"Yes'm, he is but we're taking care of him. I brought Mr. Connell some witch hazel leaves. Is he around?"

"He's in the back. He'll be out in a minute. What's wrong with your daddy?"

"Oh, he took a little spill on our porch. Didn't break anything though, thank goodness. It just shook him up some. He'll be all right again in a few days."

Through the brown store-gloom Mrs. Connell peered at Romey and me. The lace on her white dust cap quivered and her gray smile tenderly spread. "Well now, I'm glad to hear it's not as bad as what we'd been told. It'd be just awful for you children if something happened to Roy Luther."

"Yes'm, but nothing's going to."

"Is he able to eat?"

"Oh, yes'm, he eats like a horse."

Mrs. Connell sucked her papery cheeks. She removed her glasses and with the tail of her apron polished them. Squint-eyed and shrewd, she gazed at Romey and me. "When I was a youngster I lost both of my parents; they died within a week of each other and I was sent north to live with an aunt. I didn't have an easy time of it. It's terrible to be orphaned."

"Yes'm."

"My aunt was old and cranky. When I did something she thought was bad she'd force me to swallow a teaspoonful of raw quinine and send me to bed without supper."

Romey moved to stand closer to me. His eyes on Mrs. Connell's face were solemn. "She must've been a mean old lady. If I had been you I would've run away. I'm glad we haven't got any kin. I'd kill anybody that tried to make any of us swallow raw quinine. But nobody's ever going to. If anything was to happen to Roy Luther—it's not going to but if it ever *was* to—we'd just keep on living like we're living. Maybe even better. We've got it all figured out just how."

I said, "Oh, hush, Romey." And he darted a glance at me and pressed his lips and turned and stared at the row of candy jars.

Mrs. Connell returned her glasses to her face. She put her hands in her lap and resumed her rocking. Behind the polished panes of the glasses her eyes were a soft, light blue, oddly alight. Came her colorless smile again and her voice was so quiet and somehow with little flecks of pleasure and satisfaction in it, running on and on and on: "Romey, you shouldn't say like that that nothing bad is going to happen to Roy Luther. That's for God and God alone to decide. If it's His will, it will happen and no power on earth can stop it. We go when God calls us and if it's Roy Luther's time he'll go and you should be preparing yourself for it. And it's just foolish for you to stand there and say if anything happens to your daddy you'll keep on living together out there even better than you live now. You couldn't. It would be impossible. I, for one, wouldn't want to see you even try it. There are institutions for people like you. So often have I said to Roy Luther that he should lower his pride a little and accept Christian help with you children. Well, like it or not, this may be just around the corner now."

I said, "No it isn't."

Mrs. Connell inclined her head and with a finger aimlessly traced the printed flower pattern in her apron. "Oh, now, Mary Call, I know your daddy's a lot worse off than you're letting on to me. Kiser Pease was in here yesterday and told me how bad off he was. You shouldn't deceive yourself so. In the end it will just be twice as hard. You should be praying for Roy Luther's recovery but at the same time you should be preparing yourself for the worst."

To the candy jars Romey said, "You old bat."

I heard it and so did Mrs. Connell but she pretended like she hadn't, just continued to sit there rocking and smiling. And in a minute Mr. Connell came in from the back and took the witch hazel leaves from us and weighed them and paid us. I bought a package of razor blades for Roy Luther's razor and some cornmeal and five pounds of sugar. Mr. Connell said the leaves were good quality and the botanist in town would be glad to see them.

Romey said, "You're gonna see more than just leaves from us pretty soon. We're gonna start bringing you all kinds of stuff. We're wildcrafters now."

"You ain't!" exclaimed Mr. Connell and his big, rustic face flooded with rosy pleasure. "Eh, law! You going to turn wildcrafter, Mary Call? Sure enough?"

"Yes, sir," I said. "Sure enough. And so I need to know the prices you and the botanist will pay and should we look for everything or just some things?"

"Oh, look for everything," crowed Mr. Connell and hopped over to the wall and yanked down a price list from a hook. "But right now it's the time for leaves. Boneset and deer's-tongue and catnip and wintergreen and o' course the witch hazel. Then come fall you go out and dig for your roots. Bark you can go after any time. Looka here. You see this? Ginseng is bringing thirty dollars a pound right now. Thirty dollars a pound, Mary Call! And ain't either Old Joshua or Sugar Boy neither one has been prospected for years. Your mamma was the last one to do it. Folks around here've never done anything more than just piddle-diddle with 'craftin'. You got a book, Mary Call?"

"Yes, sir, we've got a book."

"If you didn't have I was going to loan you mine," said Mr. Connell and followed Romey and me outside. "Where you going to start, Mary Call?"

"Maybe on Sugar Boy," I said.

Mr. Connell propped himself up against a fuel oil drum. "Well, it's all out there. All you got to do is find it. But don't start out blind now. Study your book first and don't be in too big a hurry. What's out there'll keep. It ain't as if we had a lot of city kids pilin' in here on us every weekend rippin' the place apart like up in Virginia and Pennsylvania. We got this whole free, wide country to ourselves. And keep your eyes peeled out there. Don't go suckin' on any roots; some of 'em are deadly poison. And keep a sharp lookout for snakes. There aren't supposed to be any poisonous ones in this part of the state but you never know."

Romey said if any snakes tried to bother us he'd kick them in their behinds and Mr. Connell threw back his head and laughed.

Going home I told Romey that if he wasn't

careful he'd get his mouth cleaned out with laundry soap. "Telling Mr. Connell you were going to kick snakes in their behinds and calling Mrs. Connell an old bat. That wasn't a bit nice."

"*She's* not nice," retorted Romey with a thunderous look. "Saying there are institutions for people like us. I'd like to put *her* in an institution. Old bat."

"All right, that's enough now, Romey."

"Saying we should be praying for Roy Luther but preparing ourselves for the worst. She's hopin' he'll die. That's what *she's* praying for. The old bat."

"Romey."

"What?"

"Forget it. Just forget it. We've got other things to think about."

"All right. But Mary Call?"

"Yes, Romey."

"What if he *does* die? What will we do then?"

I said, "We'll hide it. We won't tell anybody."

Romey said, "Oh. Oh, I see."

FIVE

ILDCRAFTING IS A SIGHT EASIER TO read about than do as we all found out during the days that came then. It is not an occupation for the squeamish ones or for those who like to lie abed mornings or for anyone with weak feet or unwilling legs.

Viewed from a distance Sugar Boy's blue-tinted countenance spread up and out, joining the outlying wilderness in a smooth, benevolent sweep. Under the movement of the sun and the drifting fogs and the streaming winds, it appeared strong and silently kind but this wild and lonely primeval rock held its deceits. Its untracked trails sometimes slid steeply downward to dark, lifeless chasms tumbled thick with razor sharp boulders. Beside an icy waterfall there was a cave which most surely had harbored a large, black animal; it had left behind bits of coarse hair and a strong scent. Within a dense stand of yellow birch trees we came upon a timber rattlesnake, coiled in a puddle of sunlight. It reared its evil head and sounded its hair-raising warning and Ima Dean screamed and Romey, who had brought along Roy Luther's gun, blew its head off.

Dark birds wildly rocked in the sudden ground gusts that pervaded the upper slopes. A swarm of yellow jackets drove us from a wide, luxuriant spread of galax and Ima Dean muttered darkly over this loss. Galax was not listed in our wildcrafting book as a medicine plant but Mr. Connell's want list stated that the glossy, heart-shaped leaves were in demand by the florist in town.

We had come that morning to gather pollen—a tedious, backbreaking process, for the brightly colored dust had first to be shaken from the plant stems and then sifted through a fine cloth. Romey complained that working with it made him sneeze and asked what was it used for anyway and I said to make medicine for people who had hay fever and other allergies and he said we should have been born mountain goats instead of humans and sneezed into his pan and got his face covered with yellow floral dust.

This was a day of days. We weren't looking for the goldenseal but we found it, hidden deep within a laurel thicket, shining dark green beneath its canopy of shade. Romey was sure it was ginseng and screeched out that we were rich and ran back to the wagon for the wildcrafter's book and came back with it and we knelt and studied the pictured plate and the verbal description.

"It's ginseng," whispered Romey. "We're rich. Oh, Mary Call!"

I said, "No, I don't think it's ginseng. I think it's goldenseal. See these berries? Don't they look like raspberries? And look at the leaves. They're hairy. Look at the picture and compare it with the plants. They're alike. This is goldenseal, Romey. I'm sure of it."

"Goldenseal," whispered Romey. "We're rich. Mr. Connell wants the roots and the leaves, too. Look what a mess of it there is."

"We'll buy a car," said Ima Dean. "And all the candy we can eat and Devola some yellow shoes. A bumblebee just stung me on my ankle, Mary Call. But it doesn't hurt a bit. Not one bit."

Romey threw himself backward on the

ground and in an ecstasy of silent joy pumped his legs. Then after a minute he started to laugh and Ima Dean did, too, and they became obsessed with their laughter and kept at it so long that I had to make them stop.

The goldenseal roots came out of the ground moist and juicy, beautifully yellow in color. Romey said what were they used for and we consulted the book again and read that goldenseal is used in dyes and to make healing salves. We carried a basketful of the roots and leaves home and spread them out on an old sheet to slowly dry. Every four hours Romey turned them although the book didn't specifically say to do this.

Gathered around the lamplight we talked about how we'd spend the money. I said, "Ten dollars has to go into the money box right off. That comes first."

Ima Dean said a car was all she wanted and Romey said he'd like a book. Devola said she had changed her mind about the yellow shoes. That whatever her share was she'd give it to Roy Luther. She didn't say what she wanted him to have.

I went in and sat beside Roy Luther for a

while that night. I held his hand, so dry and frail, and talked to him:

"If you're doing any worrying about us, Roy Luther, you can stop. Today I took Romey and Ima Dean and we went up the mountain and found a big, big bed of goldenseal. The roots alone are worth dollars a pound and the leaves are worth something, too. So we earned a sizeable sum today and there's more. We only worked about half of the bed today."

Roy Luther breathed and his good eye, incredibly blue, quested my face. The light glimmered on his few white hairs.

"We forgot to reseed. The book says all good wildcrafters reseed. If they didn't do this, pretty soon all the medicine plants would die out—there wouldn't be any more. We'll do this next time we go. I had a talk with Kiser Pease, Roy Luther. He's given us this land and this house. He had me write it out on a piece of paper and he signed it and gave it to me. So now, the way I've got it figured, we're in good shape. With the money we earn from wildcrafting I aim to lay in enough supplies to last us the winter through and come next spring we'll plant and work the land. Kiser has already said he'd lend us his tractor and give us the use of his horses. And I was thinking we might even fix this house up a little. Paint some and see about getting us hot water so's we wouldn't always have to be heating it on the stove for dishes and our baths and all. Oh, Roy Luther, I do feel good about things tonight. All of us do. You feel better, don't you? You look like you do. Devola said you ate good today. Tomorrow we'll take the goldenseal to Mr. Connell and get paid for it. He'll take it even though it isn't dried. Devola wants to buy you a present but she doesn't know what. I wonder what you'd like."

Roy Luther's eyes had closed. He was asleep. I put his hand back under the coverlet and sat beside him for another minute more, just watching him breathe. The life in him is too soft now, I thought. It will go before the spring comes.

Mr. Connell acted like it made him happy to open his cash register and lay the money for the goldenseal roots and leaves in my hand. He said what were we going to do with it and I handed him my supply list.

Ima Dean, who had promised to be good and not wheedle for things impossible, left my side and tiptoed over to the jewelry counter and with real longing showing in her face gazed at a tray of gold and ruby rings. Romey went to her and took her by the hand and drew her to the front of the store. They stood in front of the soft-drink box for several minutes seriously debating. Finally they decided and Romey put the money I had given him in the slot, lifted the lid and took the drinks out. Romey uncapped them and they carried them outside and sat on the wicker bench there and happily drank.

Mr. Connell weighed pinto beans and cornmeal and, as he filled my list, ticked off each item with his pencil. "How's ye daddy, Mary Call?"

"He's some better, thank you."

Mr. Connell leaned down and got an empty cardboard carton from beneath the counter and started setting the packaged supplies in it. "Mrs. Connell and I've been meaning to drive out to pay him a little visit. How you going to get all this stuff home? You got Romey's wagon outside?"

"Yes, sir."

Mr. Connell made a trip to one of the back shelves and came back with two cans of halved peaches. "A present from me to you," he said, stowing them in the carton. "You don't have to thank me. It ain't anything. A couple of cans of peaches ain't anything."

I said, "Thank you, Mr. Connell. Roy Luther will enjoy them. I'll tell him you sent them and that you've wanted to come and pay him a visit but just haven't had the time. It's all right. He'll understand. He doesn't care much for visitors anyway. You know how it is when you're sick; visitors'll wear you out if you let them."

Mr. Connell glanced toward the curtained door that separated his store from his living quarters. He spread the supply list flat on the counter and with the heel of his hand smoothed it. "Yes, I know how it is when I'm sick. I just want people to let me alone but they come anyway. I told Mrs. Connell that Roy Luther probably wouldn't be wantin' any company. But she'll be wantin' me to drive her out to your place this evenin' or the next so you can just be on the lookout for us." He took his pencil from behind his ear, licked the point of it, tore a strip of paper from the roll at his elbow and began figuring how much I owed him.

We didn't get away without seeing Mrs. Connell. At the last minute she came from behind the curtain and with the interest so alive in her eyes but trying to hide it with her slow, waxed smile asked first about Devola and then Roy Luther. Said that it was her baking day and that she'd save a loaf of her oatmeal bread to bring out that evening or the next.

On his way to put the box of groceries in the wagon for me, Mr. Connell waddled past and said for Mrs. Connell to put a few candies in a bag for Ima Dean and Romey. She picked out the gummiest ones and followed me outside and with a little appraising flourish handed the bag to Ima Dean. She said, "Goodness, Ima Dean, you look like a little ragpicker. Your daddy should be ashamed of himself; letting you come to the store looking like that."

I was proud of my little sister then. With a grave, sweet look she accepted the candy and said thank you and didn't offer any excuse for her canvas shoes which were threadbare across the toes or for her outgrown dress.

Mr. Connell put the box of foodstuffs in the wagon and Romey turned it around and said he was ready to go if Ima Dean and I were and Mr. Connell straightened and gave me one clear look and I went across and tried to take the handle of the wagon from Romey but he wouldn't let me have it.

On the homeward trek Ima Dean threw the candy away. "It was old and dirty," she explained. "Nobody could've eaten it."

The air was warm and alive with bird song. But sweeping down through the warmth and the sun was a colder, underlying breath, very faint, just with the taste of approaching frost in it but still unmistakably there and I said to Romey that we should hurry.

He said, "No, we've got all day. All day, Mary Call."

He didn't understand me. I didn't mean that we had to hurry for that day. I meant for the days to come—the harsh winter ones that lay ahead.

It is so hard for me to write this next because it's about Roy Luther's leaving us.

I don't know how it happened or at what hour. I only knew that when I went in to him first thing the next morning he had gone. There was a congealed redness in his wide-open, unseeing eyes and he was already cold and a little stiff.

With a corner of his sheet I pressed his eyes

closed and turned him to the wall and arranged the covering over him so that it would look like he was merely sleeping and then went out and told the others that they were not to go into his room that day, not for anything.

Devola did not question this nor did Ima Dean. They ate their eggs and hoecake and asked were we going to wildcraft that day. I said no and they got out two buckets and said well then, they'd just go berrying and went out the back way and swung off down the valley in the brightening morning-gloam.

Left behind, Romey pestered me about Roy Luther saying why couldn't anybody go in to see him and why did I have his door closed and wasn't I even going to give him his bath and why were we wasting the whole day, there wasn't a thing wrong with it and what the Sam Hill was wrong with my face so clenched. That all of a sudden it looked like it was about a hundred years old and was I just going to sit around staring at the wall all morning?

I looked at him and I thought. Oh, Lord, You sure made a mistake when You put me together. You didn't give me enough strength to carry out all I'm supposed to do. I can't do this by myself.

You can see that. So now I've got to break a promise.

I said, "Romey, Roy Luther is dead."

The sun, striking through the windows, fell across his face and it twisted and his eyes ceased their questing and became so still and he said, "Oh. Oh, Mary Call."

"No carrying on now," I said. "That's one of the things I promised him. That there wouldn't be any carrying on. So if you feel like doing any don't let me see you at it, you hear me, Romey?"

Pale within his suddenly glistening face, his lips moved. "Yes, Mary Call. I hear you."

"Tonight he'll have to be buried. There's a place waiting for him up on Old Joshua. Roy Luther laid it out and dug it himself months ago. We're not to call the undertaker or the preacher. We're to do this by ourselves and keep it to ourselves. You understand me, Romey?"

His eyes, so thrust with pain and stricken, went to the wall beyond my head. "The others," he whispered. "Aren't we even going to tell the others?"

I said, "Not just now. Maybe later on in the day."

"It wouldn't be right to keep it from them,"

he said and slid from his chair and went outside and stood motionless in the sun for a long minute and then took off running, out across the fields.

Ah, I felt sorry for him then, this little brother, having to take half of this cold, terrible thing and do his mourning alone and in silence.

Throughout all of that day we moved, he and I, in a frozen, unreal style, pretending to the others to relish the berry cobbler on the noon table, more education from the root and herb book, the plans for the money we were going to make.

After noon dinner Romey built a fire under the iron pot in the back yard and Devola and I washed clothes. Ima Dean said that with the money we were going to make from our roots and herbs maybe we could buy a washing machine, one like in the Sears catalogue and maybe an electric lamp for the sitting room. She said she didn't like the oil lamps we used, that they smoked.

Romey said, "Aw, don't fuss so much, Ima Dean. Electricity costs too much; that's why we don't use it more."

They quarreled and I had to stop them.

Devola used the soapy water left over from the clothes to wash the kitchen floor and the back porch and sang while she was doing it. Twice she thought to ask me if I had bathed Roy Luther and attended to his other needs and I said yes.

One by one the hours stroked by. It turned late afternoon and Romey, half sick with dread for what lay ahead but still holding remarkably steady, got me to one side and asked me why we were keeping it from the others.

I told him because when something is finished it's easier to look back on.

He said when were we going to tell them and I said tomorrow but after that nobody else—not anybody else was to be told. Not Kiser Pease or Mr. or Mrs. Connell or anybody because if it was found out, the county people would come and take us to rear. Possibly they'd send us to an orphanage and we wouldn't be a family anymore.

For supper Devola cooked cranberry beans with ham hock and made baking powder biscuits and opened a can of the peaches. I took a tray in to Roy Luther's room and forced myself to eat what was on it. I sat beside him and tried to think words of prayer but none would come. The body under the sheet seemed smaller—looked like it had shrunk more just since that morning and I wondered how much it would weigh and thought about how we would have to tie it to the wagon with a rope unless Romey could be persuaded to walk alongside and hold it steady with his hand. From some early lesson in mortality I thought of Roy Luther saying that there would never be any understanding of death, that it was beyond people's notions and ideas and meant to be that way.

Forgotten was the threatened visit from Mr. and Mrs. Connell. They came just as the last supper dish was being wiped, Mrs. Connell stepping from their car like some spindly bird, pausing to examine the daisy beds and the patches of wild, green fern clumped along the walkway but her interest not with them at all but with us, sniffing away at our privacy and our freedom. Mr. Connell followed her up the steps and proffered their offering—two loaves of homemade oatmeal bread.

I invited them into our sitting room and Mrs. Connell drew her skirts before she lowered herself into Cosby Luther's rocker.

"Roy Luther is asleep," I said. "And I hope you don't mind if I don't awaken him. Since his fall he sleeps poorly at night."

Mr. Connell said, "Eh, law, let the man have his rest. We shouldn't have come. I told Mrs. Connell that we shouldn't but she wanted the ride."

Devola came in and crossed over to me and leaned down and whispered to me should she offer them tea or something?

Mrs. Connell smoothed her gingham arms and smiled at all of us and said, "Oh, dear no. We couldn't take a thing, thank you. We can't stay but just a minute more. You have a crack in your ceiling, Mary Call."

I said, "Yes'm, it just came. Roy Luther's been intending to fix it but he's just been so busy. He'll get around to it in a couple of days."

Mrs. Connell rocked and ironed her skirt with her hands. "I must say that I commend your father, Mary Call. Keeping you children together the way he has and never asking for a bit of out- side help." Fussing with her skirt, straightening it, she looked across the room to Romey and Ima Dean. "But pride goeth before a fall. There might come a time when he'll be glad to ask for some help."

Mr. Connell said, "Olive, for heaven's sake."

Mrs. Connell stood. She tucked her hands inside her loose sleeves. "Well, we'd better be going. You're sure Roy Luther's asleep, Mary Call? If he's even just half awake I'd like to see him just for a minute. Just a word of encouragement sometimes helps enormously, you know."

Out of the corner of my eye I saw Romey move to lay a hand on Ima Dean's hair.

I said, "Yes, he's sound asleep and I daren't try to waken him now."

Mr. Connell said, "We'll be getting on then." And stood and ushered Mrs. Connell out before him. They went past Roy Luther's closed door and out to their car and got in it and drove off.

Night had fallen. It was time to bury Roy Luther.

SIX

THE PEAKS OF THE MOUNTAINS WERE enveloped in shaggy drifts of undulating, translucent fog.

I blamed it on the mountain air, how it hurt to breathe, as Romey and I, pushing and pulling the creaking wagon, on the top of which Romey had constructed a makeshift bed to contain the trussed, shrouded figure, strained upward toward Roy Luther's final resting place on Old Joshua. The shovel we'd tied alongside him clanked a little with each turn and jolt.

At one point a raven, black and lustrous, came flapping out from a bush and flew alongside us, his hoarse *tok, tok* weird and hollow.

"Go away, bird," whispered Romey and it flew off.

We went around a fallen tree and I looked

back at Trial Valley, misted white from rim to rim, lonely as a moonscape. Lord, I thought. Oh, dearest Lord. Please don't let me give out now. It's only up a little ways further. I want to do this decent, Lord. It has to be decent so that afterward I can say to the others that it was and they'll have that much to remember at least.

From out of an empty space the raven came winging back again and lighted on top of the body in the wagon and again made his sharp, metallic cry. I shooed him with my hand and he soared upward into the somber air and disappeared.

The wagon creaked and there was the sound of our breathing. The bracken beneath our feet was dew-wet and slick. We were drowned in the dampness and the smudgy darkness.

Romey was crying but trying not to let on to me that he was. We passed under a dripping tree and a small cloud of fog streamed past us. We went over a knobby, exposed root and the wagon bumped against it and the figure on it shifted. We felt it do that and stopped. I looked back at Romey and though his face was blurred I saw his pain and fear.

"It isn't anything to be afraid of," I said. "It's all in your mind. Come on now, it isn't much further."

Hunched and desolate Romey said, "You're awful, Mary Call. *This* is awful. It shouldn't be done this way. He should have a proper burial."

"Romey, this is going to be a proper burial. Just as soon as we get him up there I'll see to it that it's proper. Come on, let's go."

"No. I'm not going any further. It's awful."

"It isn't awful, Romey. It's as good as any other kind of burial. Maybe it's even better. It's the way he wanted it. It's what I promised him."

"I don't care about that. It's awful. You're awful. You think you know everything. You're stingy. We've got the money; there's almost sixty-five dollars in the money can now. Let's take him back and tomorrow go after the undertaker and give him a proper funeral."

"No, Romey. This is the way he wanted it and this is the way it's going to be. Come on now; it isn't much further. Let's get on with it."

Romey sank to his knees beside the wagon. He put his head down on the rim of it. "No. I can't. I don't care what happens, I can't. I don't care if the county people come and get me. Let 'em. If they did I wouldn't have to look at you anymore. You old stingy gut, you."

"Be careful now, Romey. You're making me mad."

"Good. That's what I want you to do. Get mad. I want you to get mad. I hate you."

"Romey—"

"Oh, shut up!" he cried. "And stop staring at me. Haven't you got anyplace else to look?"

"Romey, come on now, Romey. I can't do this by myself. I would if I could but I can't. You've got to help me, that's all. So come on now and do it."

For a long interval he didn't move or speak. The wind above us shivered the tree branches and again the raven came back and flew around us but this time didn't alight.

Standing there on the gloomy trailway, waiting for Romey to recover, I wondered how I could be so calm—how I could just stand there in the gray darkness with the cold handle of the wagon in my hand and the cold tree moisture dripping down on me and the dead body of my father there before me and not be afraid of how grisly it all was.

It's because I'm tough, I thought. I'm so

tough that if a bear came out of the side of the mountain over there I could knock him cold without even breathing hard. And that's all and if anybody's got a better idea how I should handle this and all the other things left to me just let them come on and tell me about it but I don't hear anybody saying anything.

Back in the bushes the raven said, *"Tok. Tok."* And Romey stood up and passed one hand over his face and said, "I'll get even with everybody someday, you just watch and see if I don't. We'll go on and bury him here now but someday we'll be back to get him. Someday we'll come back here and get him and take him to the best and biggest cemetery in the whole world and we'll give him the best and biggest funeral anybody ever had. Better even than the one Napoleon Bonaparte had."

I said, "Romey, Napoleon Bonaparte didn't have a big, flashy funeral. He had a simple one. He was buried in a valley next to a stream he loved beside some willow trees."

"You're so smart," muttered Romey and leaned and straightened Roy Luther's body. He put his hands down on the rim of the wagon, one on each side of the white knob that was

Roy Luther's head and said, "Well, pull if you're going to!"

Pushing and pulling we moved upward again over bare rock and across great patches of moss and lichen and around trees and through clawing brush and after some little while of this we came to the stand of black spruce where within Roy Luther had himself prepared his burial site—a hole in the earth four or five feet deep covered with stout, broad planks left over from some carpentering job on Kiser Pease's place.

We drew the wagon up close to the edge of the grave and I said to Romey we should sit and compose ourselves before we commenced but he wouldn't be still even for one second. He was in a fever to be done with the task. He started trying to remove the planks but they were too heavy and I had to help him. When they were all laid to one side we looked down and saw that the hole itself was lined with yet more of them and in a stout voice Romey said, "It was a lot of work. It must've taken him a long time to dig down through all this rock. He must've known it was coming a long time before it did, Mary Call."

"Yes," I said.

"You bawling?"

"No."

"I didn't think you were. There's nothing to bawl about, is there?"

"No."

"All this dirt and rock piled up around. He left it here for us to pile on top, didn't he? So the animals wouldn't get to him."

"Yes, I think so."

"So that's what we'll do."

"Yes."

"So should we get on with it?"

"No, wait a minute. I want us each to say some good things now . . . the good things in our hearts that we remember about our father."

With his fair head bent reverently and his hands folded priestly, Romey stood beside the wagon, beside the body of our father and in a lilt he said, "He was gaysome sometimes before he took sick and when the notion struck him he could be as tough as whiteleather. He loved us all fair, though he never said so. He never whipped us and I was proud to have him for my daddy and now I hope he'll stay peaceful here."

"He will," I said. "He will."

Romey lifted his head and looked across at me. "Your turn now."

Beyond Romey's slight figure I saw this tree, alone and different from the rest, its branches all streamed back in one direction from the winds that had battered it year on year. It was quiet now because there was no wind but I could imagine what it looked like in a storm, bending and twisting in the gusts and the rain, resisting with all of its grit, the forces that would uproot and destroy it. It looked old and tough and the sight of it made me feel old and tough. I felt like the tree and I were related. I couldn't think of anything more to say good about Roy Luther than had already been said so I told Romey this and then together we knelt and said the Lord's Prayer and then, with some clumsiness, we loosened Roy Luther from his bindings and slid him into his grave. He went in neat.

With the shovel we then covered the grave with the planks and the loose earth and rocks and I said, "The Lord is your shepherd now, Roy Luther. Be happy with Him and don't worry about us."

Romey said, "Amen."

Going back down the mountain Romey said he believed that we had given Roy Luther a proper burial.

The next morning right after breakfast I told Devola and Ima Dean about Roy Luther. Devola took it quietly with just a little quick working in her throat but Ima Dean put her head against my skirt and cried. Then, when I tried to comfort her, she jerked away and ran out to the yard, snatched up a stick, caught her bantam rooster and tried to switch him into laying an egg. "Lay an egg!" she shouted. "That's what you're here for so go on and do it, you dumb bird, you! I'm tired of messing around with you now! Lay an egg! Lay an egg!"

I ran out and pried the stick from her hand and the wounded rooster, mortified and angered, flew up onto her head and in vengeful fury clawed her hair. She screamed and I led her back into the house. "It serves you right," I said. "I don't blame him one bit. I'd have clawed you, too."

"He hates me," she sobbed. "And after all I've done for him. If you loved me you'd go back out there and kill him!"

Solemnly Romey regarded her. "Aw, stop being such a baby, Ima Dean. Nobody else likes it either but there's nothin' we can do about it now. You want some sugar? Here, I'll give you a little sugar. Eat it now, it'll make you feel better."

Devola sat down and took Ima Dean on her lap and fed her the sugar and I talked to them then about our secret, how we were always to keep the door to Roy Luther's room closed tight and pretend, when others came and asked, that he was in it, merely sleeping, how we were never, never to breathe to anyone, not anyone, that Roy Luther had left us.

We wildcrafted that day—went back up to Sugar Boy and finished digging all the gold-enseal and planted about a hundred seeds. The sight of the 'seal bed which now lay destitute until new plants developed caused Romey to pause and anxiously look around. "There's got to be some more around here somewhere," he said. "But what if there isn't? Then what will we do?"

"Romey," I said. "Nothing's going to peter out on us. If we don't find another 'seal bed we'll take what comes. There's lots of stuff left. Lady slipper and star grass and wild ginger and just a slew of stuff. We haven't even started on any of the barks yet. I declare I don't know why you feel you've just got to have something to worry about all the time."

"We got to get the house fixed up for winter," muttered Romey.

"That isn't anything to worry about. We'll do it."

"Ha! Do you know how to fix a roof?"

"Not yet but I aim to find out."

Menacingly he thrust his lip and his chest out. "What about school?"

"What about it?"

"We going when it starts?"

"Sure."

"Won't that be dangerous?"

"It might be if you don't make any better grades in arithmetic than you did last year."

"I hate arithmetic. That isn't what I meant. I meant what about leaving Devola and Ima Dean home alone all day? What if somebody comes looking for Roy Luther and they forget and tell? You know how Devola is. She can't remember her own name unless one of us writes it down for her. What if somebody was to come while you and I were away at school and she forgot and told 'em? Then what?"

"I don't know. I'll have to figure out something."

"We got to go to school, huh?"

"Yes. We've got to go to school. You don't want to grow up ignorant, do you? And have people call you a happy pappy?"

"What's a happy pappy?"

"A happy pappy is a poor, no-account mountaineer who sits rocking on the porch of his shotgun shack all day long waiting for the mailman to bring him his charity check. He's so ignorant that's all he knows how to do. He hasn't even got sense enough to know that he's not supposed to marry his first cousin and have feebleminded children, born blind and deaf and the Lord only knows what else."

"What's a shotgun shack?"

"A shotgun shack is a shack you can shoot a shotgun through and not hit anything."

"I don't see how anybody could be happy being a happy pappy having to live in a shotgun shack with his cousin and a bunch of feebleminded kids," observed Romey.

I said, "Romey, that's what I'm trying to tell you. Happy pappys *aren't* happy. They're useless and lonely and sick. They just look happy to the people who drive by and see them sitting there rocking and grinning."

"Where'd you learn all this?"

"Miss Breathitt at school showed it to me in a magazine."

Romey hiked up one of his pants' legs and examined his ankle for insect bites. There were none but he scratched anyway. "A happy pappy. Ha. You'll never catch *me* being one. I just had an idea, Mary Call, that'll keep anybody from being tempted to try and talk to Devola and Ima Dean while we're at school. You want to know what it is?"

"Sure. Tell me about it."

"We could," said Romey, "paint up some signs that said MAD DOG or SMALLPOX or MEASLES or something like that and hang 'em on the front fence. That'd run 'em off."

I said that it was worth a thought and, pleased with himself, Romey ran around and took charge of the wagon and hollered for everybody to shake a leg, that daylight didn't grow on trees.

We didn't get the signs that said MAD DOG or SMALLPOX or MEASLES or "something like that" put up in time. Kiser Pease came riding over on his roan that night. I went out to meet him and saw that, in his fashion, he was all slicked up—yellow silk shirt closed tight at the throat with a white four-in-hand, wide, white hat, brown britches and matching jacket, some short, fancy boots. His teeth hadn't improved any though. He showed them all to me, jumped down, flicked his reins over the gatepost and said, "How be ye, Mary Call?"

On the inside of the gate I leaned against it. "Oh, I'm as peart as a cricket, Kiser."

"Ye daddy around?"

"He is but you can't see him. I'm not allowing him to have any visitors. What'd you want to see him about?"

Kiser made his nostrils twitch. "Mary Call, that's between Roy Luther and I. Now you going to let me come in and see him or not?"

"He's real sick, Kiser. Nobody gets in to see him but me. I know you don't like it, having to deal with me, but you might as well get used to it. I'm Roy Luther's spokesman now. I'm the head of the Luther family now. I'm doing all the planning and making all the decisions. Now just what is it you came over here for?"

Kiser tried to look boyish and bashful but didn't succeed. He smoothed the knot in his four-in-hand. He rearranged the brim of his hat. He reached inside his breast pocket, extracted a toothpick and stuck that between his front teeth. As the talked the pick wobbled up and down. "I said it before and I say it again: I sure would hate to be the one to marry you, Mary Call. I think you're bound for a hard time in that department. You're enough to skeer a man, standin' there all spraddle-legged with your jaw stuck out ugly. Why can't you be sweet and nice like your sister?"

I said, "Because sweet, nice girls get themselves run over by people like you. Are you back over here to see about marrying Devola again, Kiser?"

Kiser succeeded in looking bashful. "I aim to marry her, Mary Call."

"I promised Roy Luther never to let that happen, Kiser. A long time ago, when he first took sick, I promised him that. And nothing's changed. Nothing's changed. What you got there in your saddlebags? Balloons?"

"Hams," admitted Kiser with a frustrated expression. "I brought Devola a coupla hams. Lissen, Mary Call, why don't you hep me? I'd make Devola a good husband and I'd make you

Luthers a good in-law. You could come to my house every Sunday for dinner and you'd be welcomer than the flowers in May. And I'd take Roy Luther for rides in my car; he's always told me how he'd like to own a car. Wal, if he was my daddy-in-law he would, sort of. We'd all go for a little ride after dinner at my house every Sunday. Don't you think Roy Luther would like that? Wouldn't *you* like that? Sure you would."

One of us is simple, I thought. But there's no sense in being unfriendly about things. I said, "You make it sound nice but I don't know, Kiser. Car rides might scare Roy Luther. He's not used to cars. He's only ridden in a couple."

Kiser took a step and put his hand on the gate latch but removed it real quick because mine was there, holding it closed. He looked uncertain but then with a rallying display of eagerness he said, "Wal, I can fix that. I tell you what; we'll get him used to my car before we take him for rides in it. I'll bring it over here and leave it and you can show it to Roy Luther. Maybe let him sit in it for a little bit every day."

"He doesn't sit so well," I said. "Could I put some pillows in the back seat so he could *lie* down?"

"Sure, sure. It wouldn't differ about that. Whether he sits up or lays down don't—"

"Has your car got a radio in it?"

"Sure, sure. But don't go fiddlin' around with—"

"Roy Luther likes radio music. It soothes him."

"Awright, awright, let him listen to the radio."

"I've been aiming to get him a radio for his room but I just haven't been able to spare the money. How much you reckon a radio—a little one—would cost me, Kiser?"

Kiser wobbled his toothpick and let his glance flick past me to the porch. Devola had come out on it and was standing there in the soft dusk with her long hair sweetly billowed. She was singing an aimless little song.

"She just loves music," I said. "But she doesn't get to listen to any except when we go down to the General Store. How much did you say you reckoned a little radio would cost me, Kiser?"

Kiser wrenched his look back to me. "I don't know. I'll bring you a radio tomorrow when I bring the car. Lissen, Mary Call, I'm a-countin' on your help now. You talk to Roy Luther for me; you know how. He'll listen to you. Tomorrow I'll bring the car and you let him sit in it for a little bit every day—and then after Devola and I are married it won't scare him when we take him for rides."

I unlatched the gate. "That sounds reasonable. Come in, Kiser. You and Devola can do your visiting on the porch. Don't forget the hams. Want me and Devola to help you carry them in?"

. . . Late that night—later than our usual bedtime, Romey and I sat on the back steps. Romey said, "Mary Call, I don't think Kiser was crazy about Ima Dean and me hanging around while he was trying to court Devola tonight. Why'd you make us do it?"

"It was one of those necessary things," I said.

"Kiser's gonna bring his car over here tomorrow."

"Yeah."

"He wants Roy Luther to sit in it for a while every day."

"Yeah."

"I wish he could."

"So do I, Romey. So do I."

"It's too bad one of us can't drive it."

"Yeah."

"I don't think driving a car is hard. All you got to do is start her up and steer her down the road. I don't think it'd be a bit hard."

"Don't you?"

"No."

"I don't either."

"You going to try it, Mary Call?"

"Yeah."

"Tomorrow?"

"Yeah."

Romey shivered with glee.

SEVEN

THE NEXT MORNING BEFORE THE SUN was even up full Kiser brought the car. It had just been washed and waxed, every sparkling inch of it; I could tell that even from the window where I stood sipping my breakfast tea but Kiser still wasn't satisfied with its appearance. After a lot of puffed-face maneuvering to get the vehicle situated just exactly so on the grassy apron just outside our front gate he alighted and went around and got a rag from the trunk compartment and with great, vigorous swipes wiped the whole thing down again, chrome, windows, wheels and all. The squirrel tail that was attached to the hood ornament was limp with dew and he dried that with his rag and tried to make it fluff out but it wouldn't. I watched him open the back door and crawl inside and carefully massage the bright, red upholstery with the rag. Then he went to the front seat and worked that over. Then he restored the rag to the trunk compartment, looked the beginning day over, spat on the ground and started toward the gate.

"I just can't stand men who have to spit all the time," I said.

At the breakfast table Romey said, "Is he coming now?"

"Yes," I answered. "He's coming."

Romey sprinkled his oatmeal with sugar. "Let's make sure he leaves us the keys. We can tell him we'll want to lock the car every night to make sure nobody steals it. Don't worry about not knowing how to drive it, Mary Call. I think I know how. There's a guy at school can drive and he showed me how one day. It's easy. You know Miss Breathitt?"

"Yes, I know Miss Breathitt."

"The principal at school?"

"Yes, Romey."

"One day I drove her car. This guy I'm telling you about showed me how. There's not much to it."

"You drove *Miss Breathitt's* car?"

"Sure. It was easy. I drove it halfway to town."

"*You drove Miss Breathitt's car halfway to town?*" And where was Miss Breathitt while you were doing this?"

"She was licking some kids," answered Romey.

Kiser was pounding on the front door like he owned it. On my way to let him in I double checked Roy Luther's door to make sure it was locked and the key in my pocket.

Kiser said he didn't have time to come in, that he was on his way to Wilkes County to buy some hogs. He said he'd be gone for a couple of days. He pointed to the car and said there it was and did I want him to help me carry Roy Luther out to it?

I told him no, that Roy Luther had taken up with the habit of sleeping late. I told him I'd need the keys so that at night we could lock the car.

Kiser acted to me like a man on the threshold of having a Joe Blizzard fit—which refers to the irrational behavior of a legendary figure over in Harnett County noted for that. He pawed the doorsill with his booted toe and first said he didn't want anybody sitting in his car except Roy Luther. Then he changed his mind and said all of us could sit in it if we was a mind but please not to dirty it or forget to turn off the radio when we were through listening to it. He handed me the keys and with a darting look said where was Devola and I offered to go and get her from the bathroom where she was singing and splashing water but Kiser's face flushed red and he said no, he didn't have time for socializing and he backed off and hustled himself out to his car to return with a radio still in its store box. "For Roy Luther and Devola," he gabbled and fled.

Romey came to the doorway and stood beside me and we watched him humping homeward over the black, clotted fields.

"Devola's jularker," remarked Romey in a tone of ghostly discovery. "That's what Kiser thinks he is now. He's got it all fixed up in his mind that he's Devola's beau now."

The radio brought a homey touch to the sitting room. Everybody was all for taking the day off to sit around and listen to it and to playing with the car but I reminded them that there was work to be done and fired their enthusiasm for it with a promise of an afternoon ride.

Deep within a dry glen edged around with

wild blackberry bramble we found, that morning, a patch of Virginia snakeroot. At first I wasn't so sure that the pale, green plants with their slender, zigzag, jointed stems, purple at the base, weren't just weeds but Cosby Luther's wildcrafting book confirmed Romey's jubilation and in a frenzy we dug a worthwhile mound of the camphorous-smelling roots. Romey asked what were they good for and we consulted the book again but its language as regarding Virginia snakeroot gave me a headache. The words were too big.

"Well, I don't care what it does," observed Romey. "As long as we get money for digging it. Let's go now; we've earned the rest of the day off."

Swinging back down Sugar Boy we heard the juncos singing all up and down the mountainside. Spreading down the slopes the sun warmed to a noontime pitch. A towhee flitted across a fern-laced open and sang, "Time for teeeee! Time for teeeee!"

Devola was the only one to eat any lunch. She scolded the rest of us for not doing so and came trailing out of the house with her mouth full of biscuit and ham and languidly established herself in the back seat of the car and said where were we going just like we went someplace every day. Ima Dean climbed in and sat down beside Devola but then stood up and damply breathed on the back of my neck. She wanted the radio on and wouldn't shut up talking about it until it was.

Romey conceded that since I was the head of the family I should be the one to drive the car. He promised me that it would start on my first try and it did. It let out a roar like a wounded panther. It didn't move though and I hollered to Romey why and, beside me, he leaned and scrutinized all the red dashboard knobs and then the gadgetry attached to the steering wheel and suggested that I experiment and I did and the car jumped straight up and leaped backward. I don't remember Romey doing anything to my right foot but afterward he gently offered the information that he forcibly pried it from the gas pedal. I didn't hear any crash but everybody agreed there was one and when I turned around and looked back I had to say that our beautiful, old hickory fence just couldn't have collapsed without some sound.

Devola said, "The gate's hanging funny. You

really whocked it, Mary Call. I can drive. Kiser taught me how last summer, in his pickup out in the fields. Why don't you let me drive?"

The radio was twanging and bonging and screeching and Ima Dean was puffing on my neck and Romey was leaning to put his hand on my arm. He said, "It ain't nothing to faint over, Mary Call. The thing is you got to remember how much guts this car has got. It's my fault; I should have told you. You'd better let me drive; I've had more experience than you."

The car wasn't hurt. We switched places but in the driver's seat Romey found himself to be too short. He couldn't see out over the hood and he couldn't reach the gas pedal or the brake. He went to the house and returned with two pillows and that improved the situation as far as vision was concerned but there still remained the problem of his too short legs. So we switched sides again but I found that my enthusiasm for going anywhere had waned. I couldn't muster the courage to even start the car again. We turned off the radio and got out and went into the house. They were all so disappointed.

Romey and Ima Dean and I went to the airy spare room where our roots and leaves had been laid out to dry, Romey muttering how too bad it was that I was so dumb and spineless and him so deformed.

A sound coming from the front yard attracted us to the windows and we went and pulled the curtains back and looked. Devola was out there driving Kiser's car around, driving it around and around in a wide, easy circle. The noontime sun glinted on the white car and the golden loveliness of the girl in it.

"Well, for corn's sake," I said. And we went outside and stepped over the fallen fence and Romey lifted his hand, signaling to Devola to stop and she made one more graceful circle and brought the car around and came to a smooth stop in front of us. She leaned out and smiled and tenderly said, "See? I can drive. Didn't I tell you I could?"

For two days Kiser's car stayed outside our front gate and we didn't get any work done. Every time I mentioned the word they all groaned and accused me of being a slave driver and a killjoy. Once Romey persuaded Devola to drive the car clear up to the main road and back though I shouted for them not to, ordered them to work, reminded them that winter was coming. They said they didn't care about winter, that they'd deal with it when it came. The house radio sat neglected on the table in the sitting room. They played the car one and blew the car horn and from morning to night had a fine time riding around and around in the car. Finally, though, they had to give it up because it ran out of gas. Ima Dean howled and wailed and I lost my temper and shook her and Devola pulled her away from me and the two of them ran off down the road toward Old Joshua.

"They didn't take any lunch," Romey said. "They'll stay up there all day without anything to eat. Devola hasn't got sense enough to know when to come home."

"Good," I said. "Let them starve to death. I don't care. Where's the book?"

"In the wagon. Ima Dean's only five, Mary Call. You got to remember that."

"I remember it. I remember I'm only four-teen, too, and I've got the worry of all of you on me and I don't see anybody killing themselves helping me. While you frittered like jackasses all day yesterday and the day before I was out there working like a dog for you so don't go telling me what I've got to remember. I remember plenty and none of it good. Get the dishpan."

Romey shuffled his feet and released a sigh. "Well, I'm sorry you've got the worry of *me* on your mind. I didn't ask anybody to fix it this way though. I didn't ask to be born. I wish I hadn't've been."

"Yeah? Well, maybe you'll fall off the mountain today and kill yourself and be out of your misery. Get the dishpan."

Romey thrust his jaw out. "Get it yourself. I'm not your slave. You're the hatefulest person alive, Mary Call. If Roy Luther was alive you wouldn't treat us like you do."

"Just get the dishpan, Romey, and shut your trap. I haven't got any time to stand around here this morning and listen to you whine. We've got work to do."

Romey darted over to the stove, made a furious appraisal of the breakfast leftovers, snatched a crumbled paper bag from the hook where Devola kept them, stuffed four corn dodgers and two pieces of cold, fried ham, whirled, and ran out the door. His feet barely touched the ground as he sped down the path in the direction of Old

Joshua, screaming for Devola and Ima Dean to wait for him.

By myself I gathered richweed pollen that day. Alone on a dry, open slope I worked my way through dense weeds higher than my head, gathering the green-yellow heads into bunches, bending their stems to the piece of organdy spread out over the dishpan, shaking the flowers to rid them of their precious grains. At one point in this process I was horrified to feel my eyes fill with tears and I cussed, I think. Some life for a girl, I thought. Out here alone on this blasted mountain working myself to a frazzle, for what nobody knows. Lord, I've said it before and I'll say it again: You sure made some mistakes when You made me. Surely to my soul I must have moss growing in my head where my brains should be. Nobody but a poor dement would do what I'm doing, hiding my old dead daddy over there on Old Joshua. Taking me on three snot-nosed kids to raise. If I had the sense of a rabbit or even half that much I'd just take off across that bald over there and go down the other side of it and just keep right on walking and never look back. They'd make out all right without me.

Probably even better. The county people'd come and get them. Maybe not Devola but the other two. Kiser'd probably get Devola.

Out there on Sugar Boy that morning those were the thoughts that bitterly filled my head and had not a squadron of hornets attacked me, zooming down from their paper nest hanging like a lantern from a tree branch, puffing me all up sick and poisonous with their venom, I might have gone on and deserted. By accident I brushed the hornets' nest with a stick I had picked up for no reason and they acted with savage efficiency. I received two stings on my face and three on my arms.

I swelled up like a toad and my heartbeats slowed to painful thumps and I was sick all along the homeward trail.

My family was nowhere about. Kiser Pease was sitting in Roy Luther's chair on our front porch, rocking himself. His pickup truck was parked outside the gate; in the caged back end of it there was a pig. I reeled up the steps but Kiser didn't stand up. He just set the rocker down hard and leaned forward and peered at me and said, "Eh, law! What you gone and got yourself into now, Mary Call? What you got there?"

"It's pollen," I said, clutching my precious burden.

"What's it for?"

"For a while," I said. "Kiser, do I look sick to you?"

Kiser scrutinized me. "Wal, yes."

"That's because I am," I said. "If you were a gentleman you'd get up and let me have that chair."

Kiser got up and let me have the chair. He went over and sat down on the top step. He took a toothpick from his breast pocket and stuck it between his front teeth. "While I was waitin' for some of you'uns to come back I took the freedom of tryin' to get in to speak to Roy Luther but his door wuz locked."

Beneath the slick inner sole of my shoe I felt the reassuring lump of the key to Roy Luther's room. "Yes," I said. "I keep it that way."

"So then," said Kiser, wobbling his toothpick. "I went around outside and looked in his window. Somebody left the blind open a little ways. He ain't in there, Mary Call."

"He ain't?"

"No."

My heart, which had been limping along at a

sluggish, heavy pace due to the hornet stings, suddenly developed a cruel torturous vigor. I had to wait for it to quit lurching and while I was waiting Kiser looked at me and wobbled his toothpick.

I said, "Well, I haven't jailed him. He comes and goes as he pleases. Probably right now he's just gone off somewhere with Romey and Ima Dean and Devola. They'll be back directly."

"I brought Devola a pig," said Kiser with a dogged expression. "You'uns can slaughter him come the first cold snap. But the main reason I'm a-hangin' around is to talk to Roy Luther. I just know *you* haven't like you said you would so I'm a-gonna do it myself."

I couldn't persuade him that I had—I couldn't persuade him to go home. He wouldn't budge. The pig, which was a young one, made oinking noises and Kiser, chewing on his toothpick, said I was wasting my time trying to scare him off with looks. I went inside and vomited again and looked at my face in the mirror. It was hideously swelled and throbbing with fever and so were my arms. It'd serve them right if I died from this, I thought. Then they'd find out who was hateful and a slave driver.

Through the autumnal mists they came straggling home eventually, my three ingrates: Ima Dean, dirt-streaked and briar-scratched and crying; Romey, sheep-faced in the lead; Devola with her head in the clouds and aimlessly singing.

Kiser stayed on the step where he was. I went out along to meet them. In a voice loud enough to carry I said, "Where's Roy Luther?"

"He's back there," howled Ima Dean. "Romey hit me on my head, Mary Call, and it hurt!"

Romey said, "Oh, shut up, Ima Dean. Just shut up. All day long all you've done is blubber and bawl. Just be thankful I didn't twist your head clear off your neck. Next time I will."

I said, "Romey, if I were you I'd just watch out for my own head because yours is in some pretty grave danger right now. Get to the house, all of you. Where'd you say Roy Luther was?"

Romey's eyes, suddenly fearful and suddenly ravaged with a terrible, enshadowed anxiety, went keenly past me to Kiser who had risen and come down to the bottom porch step. With exquisite care he said, "He's back there. We couldn't get him to come home. He's pretty disgusted at Ima Dean and I don't blame him. Bawl baby. All she does is bawl."

Nobody asked what was wrong with me. They went past me and past Kiser's white passenger car and started past the pickup but the pig in its back made them pause and look. Kiser came loping out and said the pig was a present for Devola and Devola put her face to the slats and yearningly said wasn't it sweet and Kiser tremored and sprang up, straight up over the topmost slat to the cage and quiveringly handed the pig down. Devola cuddled him, carried him into the house, Romey and Ima Dean trailing.

I felt kind of sorry for Kiser then but he wasn't offering me any pity so I didn't offer him any. I just said, "Roy Luther's had his fill of sitting in your car, Kiser. You'd best take it home now."

"No," said Kiser. "I'll leave it here. Devola can drive it if she wants to. She knows how. I learned her last summer."

"It's out of gas," I said.

"Wal," said Kiser and gloomily shuffled around to the front of the pickup and got a five-gallon can that was filled with gas and took it over to his car and poured all of it into the tank.

"Devola should get her a license to drive. I'll take her into town and hep her git it whenever she feels like goin'."

Well, I thought, you don't look a gift horse in the mouth. Maybe they're tired of playing with the car and it might just come in handy. "Tomorrow," I said, "Romey and I have to go register for school so tomorrow'd be a good day for it. You can take us as far as the school and then go on. So you come early tomorrow morning, Kiser. I'll have Devola ready."

"Do you think she liked the pig, Mary Call?"

"Oh, yeah. She was crazy about it. She likes all animals: chickens, pigs, cows, all animals. She's a fool about cows—she loves milk but we never have any."

Kiser looked at me. "Awright, I'll bring her a cow. What time you reckon Roy Luther'll be comin' home?"

"Oh, he may not be back for a day or two, Kiser. He's queer in the head now. But don't worry. When he does come back I'll talk to him for you. I sure will. I promise you. Will you bring the cow tomorrow or when?"

"Tomorrow," sighed Kiser and got in his pickup and drove off.

Romey and Devola and Ima Dean built a pen for the cow that evening. They had to use part of our yard fence to do it—took two whole sections of it out and moved it around to the back.

I was too sick to help. Roy Luther's favorite simple for hornet stings—roots of marshmallow combined with lard—weren't helping me much. I lay on my bed nursing my fever and swellings, listening to them chatter and hammer. And presently Romey came in and sat beside me and said, "We're sorry, Mary Call."

I said, "Shut up and get out of here."

"We're all just terrible sorry. You're not going to die or anything like that, are you?"

"No, I'm not going to die or anything like that but it'd serve you right if I did. Go take a bath. You stink. You're giving me the headache."

Romey inched his chair forward. He bent and put his hand on my cheek. It smelled like wet dirt and chicken manure, but felt wonderful. In a tender voice, so tender, like Devola's, he said, "You're not hateful to us, not ever. We're the ones that're hateful to you and we're sorry. We know you're the boss and we know that's the way it's got to be. Tomorrow morning we're going to get up at five o'clock and go wildcrafting and we're going to work at it all day. You won't have to go with us. We want you to stay here and rest and get well. We'll do all the work. You won't have to even move a muscle. All you got to do is lay here and rest and get well and think of some more orders you want to give us."

"We have to go and register for school tomorrow," I said. "Keep quiet or get out of here." But he wouldn't go. He continued to sit there, softly stroking my hair until I went to sleep and dreamed that I myself married Kiser Pease and all of us went to live in his house with the yellow kitchen and the plentiful hot water and all our problems were overnight-solved.

EIGHT

THE COW THAT KISER DELIVERED TO US was a Hereford—red with a mottled-white face. Kiser said she was hardy like all of her breed—that she could be turned loose and allowed to forage for herself. He had brought along a salt lick and set that down in her pen. He didn't ask me if I knew how to milk her so I was spared having to say that I didn't. He did say that the milk from her might taste a little like wild carrot because that was her favorite summer food. With a dry, sidelong look he said he hoped I'd drink my share of it, that it might improve my looks and personality. He asked where would I store the surplus and I said in our root cellar since we didn't have a refrigerator and he blinked and jerked back and turned and ran out to the pickup and busied himself with something in the front seat.

Devola was loitering. First she put her hair up and then she took it down and then she had to wash it again.

I was obliged to invite Kiser in for a cup of tea and he accepted and while he was trying to drink it I talked to him candidly. I told him that he'd better have Devola back home not later than three o'clock, that Roy Luther might be queer in the head but he still knew how to use his shotgun. I told him he'd better not try anything funny like running Devola off to the judge with marriage in mind. I said to him that Ima Dean had her orders to watch every move and report every word.

Kiser was in a claphat mood to get going but he argued with me about taking Ima Dean along: "Now lissen, Mary Call. Devola and me are just goin' into town to get her a driver's license. That's all. We're goin' right in and comin' right back. Except for dinner. Come noon, if we've had to wait or somethin' like that I'll want me a nice dinner and I shore won't let Devola stand outside hungry on the sidewalk and wait for me. I'll take her inside and feed her, too. But I shore didn't bargain to take no little kid along today now."

"Oh, Ima Dean doesn't eat much," I said. "She's never eaten in a cafe. Get her some ice cream. That'll keep her quiet. She likes ice cream. Besides it's part of Devola's job to mind Ima Dean. I or Romey can't take her with us when we register for school."

Kiser licked his teaspoon though there wasn't anything on it to taste. "Mary Call, I want to speak to Roy Luther. You goin' to let me this morning?"

"Kiser, I would. I'd be glad to. But Roy Luther's not here this morning. He's root digging up on Joshua."

"Root diggin', huh?"

"Yes."

"I thought you said he was queer in the head now."

"He is. I have to tell him what to do. I told him to go up there and dig some roots and so that's what he's doing."

Kiser licked his spoon again and then he shoved the bowl of it into his mouth and bit it. "Mary Call, between now and nightfall today I aim to see Roy Luther and speak to him. I'm a-gonna do it if I have to hog-tie him and if you get in my way you and I might have a little mite

118

o' trouble. So you can be thinkin' about that while Devola and me are gone to town. You just get it clear in your head that I aim to speak to Roy Luther today and there ain't nothin' on this earth a-gonna stop me. Not even you. You got that straight now?"

He meant it, I could see that and what I was going to do about it addled me so that I forgot to tell him Romey and I wanted to ride down as far as Relief Road which is where you turn from the main one to get to the school-house and Romey and I had to walk every step of the way.

As we jogged along Romey had some pretty dark comments to make: "People's sins always catch up with 'em," he said.

"Oh, for corn's sake, Romey, I haven't committed any sin."

"You think burying Roy Luther up on Old Joshua the way you did wasn't a sin?"

"No. Burying him the way *you* wanted to bury him with an undertaker and a preacher would have been. A bought funeral is nothing but a gouge. Roy Luther said so to me and I believed him. Undertakers and preachers don't make people get to heaven any faster if they're going. They just make it look that way to the people who're left behind. These hills are full of people who've been buried in private. There isn't a thing wrong with it as long as there's been no foul play done. Shut up and help me think now."

"About what?"

"How to get shed of Kiser Pease. He's useful to us a little bit but he's dangerous, too. If he knew Roy Luther was dead and buried he'd have all of us except Devola in a county home so fast we wouldn't even have time to breathe twice before it happened."

"He wants to marry Devola."

"Sure he does but he's not going to because I promised Roy Luther never to let that happen. Devola's never going to be anything but a child, Romey. Roy Luther knew that. I promised him to keep her with me always and that's what I'm going to do. I don't trust Kiser Pease. There isn't any goodness in him. He's all cheat and sneak."

Romey picked up a rock and chunked it hard into a roadside stand of flowering thistle and a cloud of purple, silky down erupted into the warming air. "I could take Roy Luther's shotgun and blow Kiser's head off," he suggested.

I said, "Romey, why are you always talking about twisting somebody's head off or blowing somebody's head off? That's what earned people like us the reputation we've got."

"What reputation?"

"The reputation we've got for being ignorant and crazy. That's what people who live outside of here say about us. That's what the flatlanders say about us; that we're ignorant and crazy and don't want to be any other way. You remember Roy Luther telling us that; it's one of the things he talked about the strongest. How people think we're crazy because we're always wanting to fight and blow people's heads off. A gun never settled anything, Romey. Brains are what solves things, the brains God gave us. What we've got to do is learn to use them and be smarter than other people. There's a civilized way to deal with Kiser if I can just think of it."

Romey stopped walking, knelt in the road, and removed his shoe. There was a hole in the sole of it the size of a quarter. Dismally he surveyed it. "I should get me a new pair when we go to the General Store next time but I don't see how we can afford it. I sure hate being so poor all the time."

I said, "Yeah, well there are worse things I can tell you. Ignorance is one of them. Of course, if you're not ignorant you won't be poor, not for long anyway. Put your shoe back on, Romey, and let's go. We'll get you a new pair when we take our roots and stuff to Mr. Connell tomorrow. Come on, let's go."

Miss Fleetie Breathitt, who was the principal of our school as well as my teacher and sometimes Romey's, said she was glad to see us two Luthers again. She wondered what had happened to swell me up so and I told her about the five hornet stings and she gasped and said I should be in bed, that more people died from insect bites than from snake bites every year, it was a matter of medical statistics.

I said I was too tough to die from anything as trivial as five hornet stings and she snapped her glossy eyes. "How is Roy Luther, Mary Call?"

"He's fine. Probably better than he's ever been. Miss Breathitt, if possible I want to work in the cafeteria again this year for my meals and Romey's big enough, too, now. Will there be a place for us?"

Miss Breathitt took a bite of her pencil eraser

and said yes, she'd arrange it.

I said, "Before I go for today, Miss Breathitt, can you tell me please how old the Great Smoky Mountains are? Romey asked me and I didn't know but I sure would like to. It's kind of embarrassing to live right on top of something and not know about it."

Miss Breathitt took another bite of her eraser. She looked at me straight and I saw banners in her eyes waving. "Oh, my. Well, let me see. Let me see if I can remember my geology. If I remember correctly the Great Smoky Mountains were raised at the end of the Paleozoic era, probably prior to the Cambrian time which is the oldest period of the Paleozoic era."

"How long ago was this?"

"Oh, my," said Miss Breathitt. "Geologists differ in their speculation but many authorities in this field agree that these mountains were already in existence prior to the Pre-Cambrian time. So reckoning from this perhaps they occurred some two billion, five hundred million years ago."

Someday, I thought I'm going to be as smart as she is and be able to spout out all that stuff when people ask me and play the piano for assembly and fix my hair like that, white on the tips, and have little kids afraid of me.

Miss Breathitt had risen and gone to her skitter-scatter bookshelves. "Somewhere in all of this I have a book on mountains. Oh, here it is. Would you like to borrow it, Mary Call?"

"Yes, ma'am, I sure would. I'll take good care of it. I aim to buy some home books pretty soon. We're wildcrafting now. I didn't tell you that, did I?"

The banners in Miss Breathitt's eyes snapped and crackled. "No. How wonderful."

Miss Breathitt thought a lot of things wonderful. Birds, air, the first snow, curiosity, cleanliness. She was always carping about cleanliness. She argued that it was truly next to godliness, that it made it easier for us to bear ourselves and others to bear us, that it was a source of moral strength. She said that being clean was one of the wonderful things in life.

Friends were another thing Miss Breathitt believed in and thought wonderful. Friends, she said, improved talents and happiness and all of us should take care to make some.

This last advice of hers was good, I thought,

if you aren't hiding anything. If you are you'd best leave friends alone.

On the schoolground Alma and Gaither Graybeal from over in Pigtail Hollow were waiting for Romey and me, both of them eager to be school-term friends again. They asked could we go home with them, that their daddy, who owned and operated the only steam-run molasses mill in the county, had just started a fresh cooking that day and wouldn't some of that foamy sweetness taste good?

Able to taste it, I said it would but that we didn't have the time for any visiting and took Romey by the arm and forced him away from the temptation of saying we'd come another time. Maybe there would be other times when we could all stand around the steaming vat of the Graybeal farm and watch the rich cane juice being filtered through burlap and have Mr. Graybeal scoop us up bowls of the warm, glistening syrup and laugh at our enjoyment.

I could see that it hurt Romey, our having to rid ourselves of the Graybeals' friendship and I wanted to say to him to never mind, that it was only a temporary thing. Then I thought about this choice of words and I couldn't say them because Roy Luther, lying in his grave up on Old Joshua, wasn't temporary. He was as permanent as anything gets to be and though the Graybeals weren't snoopers and only rode over to Trial Valley once or twice a year, there would be risk in their visits. They might come on the wrong day. Roy Luther's locked door might arouse suspicion. Ima Dean or Devola might slip of the tongue. Anything could happen.

On the way home Romey, with his face newly bereft and lonely, talked in a forced hearty way about school which would begin on the following Tuesday and how much work we had to do before the long, deep winter would whip into Trial Valley.

"When it happens we got to be ready for it, Mary Call."

"Yes."

"The cow'll help a lot."

"Yes. A lot."

"And when the pig gets bigger and fatter we can kill him and eat him."

"Yes."

"You thinking about something, Mary Call?"

"Yes."

"What?"

"What I'm going to do about Kiser. Somehow I've got to get rid of him. I've been thinking that I might tell him I wanted to marry him. That might do it. He'd rather have both lungs cut out than marry me. If I pretended that I was crazy for him all of a sudden that might do it. He thinks I'm the ugliest, meanest little twerp ever lived. I think I'm going to declare my love for him today; it's the only thing I can think of that would scare him off. If you were Kiser, Romey, and I came bleating and panting around you and said that it had just come to me that I was mad in love with you, what would you do?"

Romey turned a brisk and serious look at me. "Would you look like you look now?"

"Sure. Maybe worse."

"Then I'd run," said Romey and didn't laugh or even smile to soften this moment of honest language.

A car going in the same direction went past us but didn't slow. It had a Georgia license plate. We left the road and cut through a meadow of Queen Anne's lace which now in late summer was curled and withered and prickly with age. The air was clear and tart. Overhead the sun burned bright but there was the taste of frost and in our path swirls of fluttered leaves.

From the distance, looking out and across the winding shine of Trial Creek to the bluemisted knob which was host to the Luther home I experienced a pang. It's falling down, I thought, and I don't know how to stop it and maybe before I find out I'll be ready for a grave up on Old Joshua myself.

Devola and Ima Dean had come ahead of us and were there on the porch waiting for us as we climbed the steps. Devola had the oinking pig in her lap. Kiser's car was parked in its earlier place but Kiser was nowhere about. Ima Dean, with a huge bag of yellow and red wrapped candies, was sitting on the floor, delving into it, making one big pile and three smaller ones.

I said, "Romey, go out and turn off that car radio. I can't hear myself think. Where's Kiser, Devola?"

Devola stroked the pig. "We had to leave him in town. He got sick."

"What do you mean, he got sick?"

Devola turned her tender smile. "A truck ran over him, Mary Call."

"What truck?"

"I don't know. Just a truck."

"He wasn't looking where he was going," supplied Ima Dean. "It was a big truck, the biggest one I ever saw. They said it broke both of his legs and maybe his jaw."

"Who said that?"

"Some doctors. Two doctors came and looked at him and that's what they said. Then they took him away."

"Took him away where?"

"I don't know. To a hospital."

"Did they ask you any questions?"

"No."

"They didn't ask you and Devola your names?"

"No."

"Did anybody look at you?"

"No. They just looked at Kiser."

"Did Kiser say anything to you?"

"No. He couldn't. His jaw was broke."

"Then what happened?"

"Then," said Ima Dean, "we went and got in Kiser's car and came home."

Kiser was in the hospital and out of our way for a while. We had land, a house, a cow, a pig, and a car. We had found a way to make money.

We were together. Anxiety and apprehension should have been the furthest things from my mind. But because I am a pessimist and must always keep sticking my tongue in pessimism the way you do a sore tooth I couldn't help thinking that it was all too easy. Things just aren't this easy for people, I said to myself. Something or somebody is bound to come and spoil it. I don't know what or who but it'll come so you can just get yourself ready for it.

A cloud shadow, drifting the breadth of Trial Valley, spread across the inscrutable face of Old Joshua.

NINE

Now there was this time of in-between and during its span an elusive old foe—money—drew us into its merciless mesh and was our master.

I will confess that I was an unwilling partner in this last. Each morning even before the dawn came slipping, cold now and wet with gray, wraithy fog, I routed them and stood over them, prodding them to stand up and open their eyes, to dress, wash, eat, and gather up the tools and go out and do what had to be done.

Sleepy and ill-humored, shivering with the cold, they would shamble out and set their feet one in front of the other and we would start off down the valley, the wagon in tow, the wheels of it creaking and rattling with every step and turn. I would try to get them to sing or talk, do anything to raise their spirits, but they remained sullenly silent. At that hour they hated me and I hated myself, knowing how I appeared to them—a pinch-faced crone, straggle-haired, bony, ragged, too desperate for anyone with only fourteen years on them but still driven by a desperation that was unholy and ugly. Straggling up the mountainside through the sodden, gloomy daybreak I would see the beauty of it all around me, free for the looking and the listening. Surely, I would think, the Lord is here. Roy Luther believed that He was and I believe it, too. He is here and watching over everything, helping it. I believe that. But if this is so where is my share of the help, answer me that. There isn't going to be any help for me, is there? There's just going to be me and this mountain and that other one over there and these three children and whatever good we can make for ourselves.

Within a damp, sheltered wood of Fraser firs and rhododendron and laurel we dug lady slipper root (Noah's ark) and from the dry desolation of a waste area we dug the spindle-shaped root of the yellow dock which is a plant of the buckwheat family. We felled young, wild cherry trees and skinned them of their bark, peeling back the smooth, reddish-brown outer layers to reach the green ones underneath.

Sugar Boy's stones and gravelly trails finished Romey's shoes. Late of an afternoon we loaded all of our wild harvest and Devola drove us to Mr. Connell's General Store and we bought him a new pair, sturdy brown with black, cleated soles.

Mrs. Connell came gliding out from behind her house quarter's curtain to watch the shoe buying and then the selection of foodstuffs which had to be done so carefully. She looked hard at Devola who was wandering up and down the aisles and said, "Whose car is that you children are driving, Mary Call?"

"It belongs to Kiser Pease. He's letting us use it while he's in the hospital."

"Does Devola have her driver's license?"

"Kiser took her to get it the day he had his accident, yes'm."

Mrs. Connell sucked her powdery lips. "How's Roy Luther?"

"He's better but still not able to visit with people. Oh, that reminds me; he needs razor blades again this time. Will I have to buy the whole packet or can I buy just one?"

"They only come in packets of five," said Mrs. Connell. But Mr. Connell, coming to the center where we were standing, opened the box of blades and took one of them out and added it to the parceled pile of shoes and beans and sugar and tea and flour which took nearly all of our wildcrafting money.

Mr. Connell counted out in my hand what cash we had left and said he was sorry it wasn't more and Romey, though I pinched his arm warningly, exchanged a large stare with Mrs. Connell and said he sure hated to see other people enjoy the misery of others. Mrs. Connell sniffed and touched her papery cheeks with her fingertips and said when she came to see Roy Luther next time she was going to speak to him about Romey's manners. In a swish of lilac scent she went past us and stood outside and watched us load our supplies and drive off.

"I'm gonna fix her," promised Romey. "I'm gonna do it the very next time she comes sniffing and smelling around our house. What I'd like to do is blow her old head off but I don't want people to think I'm crazy so I'll have to think of something else. Don't worry; I will. I'll think of something to fix her."

He spent all one evening painting a sign that said POX in red letters and this he nailed to the front gate.

"What kind of pox?" I asked.

"Just pox," was his dark-browed answer. "She can take her pick what kind I wish on her."

"If we had pox and Miss Breathitt got wind of it she'd have the health people out here," I said. "Then we'd be in trouble sure enough. For us Mrs. Connell is too dangerous a woman to do any messing around with, Romey. You let me handle her when she comes. You just keep your mouth shut. Don't look at her and don't say anything to her. Go out and take the sign down now; we don't need it."

He obeyed me—took the sign down and came back in and until bedtime talked about school and medicine plants and money and what he was going to do when he grew up and where he was going to live which sure wasn't going to be anywhere around Trial Valley or even in the state of North Carolina. He had me go with him out back to the cowpen and hung on the rail, gazing at our prize, and said there wasn't anything to milking once you got the hang of it.

From some of the cow's surplus milk which did, in fact, taste slightly of wild carrot as Kiser had said it would, Devola had made some cottage cheese and Romey ate a bowl of that sprinkled with sugar and declared it to be better than ice cream. But he hadn't forgotten his promise to fix Mrs. Connell. Within him all the while there was a scheme brewing, aided and abetted by an old, raunchy, rancid-smelling black bearskin, complete with head and feet and arms which was the property of Kiser Pease.

Ima Dean reported Romey's acquisition of the skin: "There's a bear in Romey's closet, Mary Call."

"Is there? Well, I'll look at him after a while. Right now I'm studying."

"He's not alive though. He's dead."

"Is that so?"

"Romey says he's going to stuff him."

"That's nice."

"And stand him up in the road."

"Really?"

"Then when Mrs. Connell comes she'll be

scared and run off."

"That'll be nice."

"Does reading hurt your eyes?"

"Sometimes."

"Is it hurting them now?"

"A little."

"Then why are you doing it?"

"Because I don't want to be ignorant."

"You wish I'd go away, don't you?"

"Yes."

"Then I'll go," said Ima Dean and skipped away to seek Devola. They played jacks on the front porch until it got too dark to see.

On the way to school the next morning— walking because gas for the car cost too much— I did fleetingly remember the bearskin hanging in Romey's closet and did open my mouth to ask him about it, but just then Mr. Graybeal pulled up alongside us and told us to hop in, and it was so crowded in the cab of his truck and Alma and Gaither were quarreling over whose turn it would be that day to help out after school in the molasses mill, and I was already tired from having studied so late the night before and from having already been out that morning with Romey gathering lobelia plants, that the question slipped away from me and never got asked.

In Home Economics class that day we made applesauce cake. Mine turned out swaybacked.

During Civics a fat girl, who didn't want to be that way, fainted and had to be carried to Miss Breathitt's office, there to languish until the last bell rang.

Romey and I walked home in a body-chilling rain. As we slogged along Romey angrily said it wouldn't have hurt to accept a ride with the Graybeals for as far in our direction as they went anyway. "Mr. Graybeal thought you were crazy, turning him down like you did," he said. "Why did you?"

I said, "Romey, we can't be friends with the Graybeals. We can't be friends with anybody. You know that and you know why."

In the wet afternoon twilight Romey's face appeared suddenly old and bereaved. "Is it gonna be like this forever? It is, isn't it?"

I started to say that forever was a long time but then I thought, There's no comfort in that fool. And I couldn't think of anything that *was* comforting so didn't say anything.

The wind was eye-whipping and the rain was pounding at us. We left the road and sloshed through the meadow of Queen Anne's lace, sodden and bent heavy. Romey said his new shoes would be ruined for sure and sat down on a rock and took them off and tucked them inside his wet shirt.

Mrs. Connell tried to come visit us that night. Just after the lights of day had started to lower and the night to close in, I saw the headlights of her car, weaving faint yellow, way down on the lower end of the valley road. "It's Mrs. Connell," I said to Devola, who was standing beside me. "I remember the sound of her car from before."

Devola put her hand to her mouth. "Roy Luther's door. I didn't close it after I cleaned his room today."

We both ran inside to close the door and to make other things look natural and unsuspicious. Devola set a pair of Roy Luther's shoes crooked in front of Cosby Luther's rocker in the sitting room. She draped one of his old sweaters across the back of the chair. In the bathroom I laid out his razor and a wadded towel.

We ran back out and stood on the porch. In a whisper Devola said, "She's still coming. Will we tell her Roy Luther's asleep?"

"Yes."

"Will she believe us?"

"I don't know."

"Should I make her some tea?"

"No. Yes."

"Look," said Devola. "Look, Mary Call. She's changed her mind. She's turning around. Look at her. Look. Why is she going so fast the other way now? Look at her."

I looked and saw the reason. About fifty yards from our gate there had appeared in the road a huge, black bear with a brute of a face and wide open arms. He wasn't making a sound and he wasn't moving. He seemed rooted to the center of the road, the black shadows curling around his feet and his head.

Later on I said to Romey that he shouldn't have used our pillows to make the stuffing for the bear. "We'll never get the stench out," I said.

He said, "I liked to died laughing, watching that old bird fly out of here. The wheels of her car didn't hardly touch the ground. She sure enough thought old bruin was after her. I wish I could have made him chase her. I wish I could have made his jaws pump. Wouldn't that have been funny if I could have made his jaws go up and down? Did you see how fast she went around him? Suhwoooooooooosh!" said Romey. "That was the funniest thing I ever did see. You don't think she'll be back, do you?"

"Probably."

"Tonight? You think she'll come back tonight?"

"No, I don't think tonight but she'll be back sometime."

With both hands Romey explored the shape of his head. "It's not easy to hide things, is it, Mary Call?"

"No."

"I wish we didn't have to. You want some cottage cheese? It's good with sugar sprinkled on it."

"No, thanks. I just want to go to bed."

Romey helped himself to a bowl of cottage cheese. "What will we do next time she comes back?"

"I don't know. We'll have to think of something. Maybe winter will come early. That'll keep her away for a while at least."

TEN

On the 30th day of October the dreaded winds that breed along mountain turrets around Trial Valley, exploding to life with the first real temperature change, came barreling into Trial Valley. Shivering the bare branches, pounding and shrieking, it sent the snakes and the groundhogs and all other wildlife scurrying to burrowed refuge. The tall, stout teasels out beside the cow enclosure bent low in its wake. Some of the loose shingles on our roof were pried and went sailing off into the raging air. Romey and I climbed up and had a look at the bald places. What was left seemed to me to be a mighty thin defense.

"We should have fixed these places weeks ago," I said. "We knew this was coming."

The wind was pulling at our hair and clothes.

Romey wiped his eyes with his sleeve but they immediately watered again. His nose and lips and hands shone blue with the cold. "Should have, should have," he retorted. "We've been running as fast as our danged legs'll carry us. What d'ya think we are anyway? Centipedes? If somebody was to stick ten sticks of dynamite under each of us every morning at sunrise we couldn't run no faster. Dig, dig, dig and pick, pick, pick and chop, chop, chop some more. Oh, what a life. And what a country. Anybody'd live out here has to be plumb queer in the head. I hate it. You just wait. I'm making a few plans. I'm gonna get outa here. I'm gonna go so far away from here none of you'll ever see me again or hear from me. And where I'm going I'll never look at another root or another leaf or another piece of bark."

I said, "Never mind all that. This isn't any easier for me than it is for you. Go down the ladder and get me the hammer and some nails."

"Go down the ladder and get your own hammer and nails!" he shouted. "You're the one wants this danged roof fixed! I don't care if it blows clean to Virginia!"

He was afraid and I was afraid, for winter in

all its savage efficiency was upon us though the calendar didn't say so and our preparation for it had fallen some short of the planning.

Ropes of onions hung from pegs in my room and Romey's. In the root cellar, embedded in layers of clean sand, there were beets and carrots. The cellar's bins brimmed with winter squash and potatoes. A straw-lined hole in the back yard was crammed to the top with fresh cabbages; in the winter, when the ground wasn't too hard, we would take those up, one by one, and boil the brittle, snow-white leaves with red peppers and fat meat. All mountaineers know about this tasty dish.

There was what I considered to be a near-comfortable surplus of staples: dried pinto beans, flour, cornmeal, sugar, tea. There were three slabs of salt-encrusted white pork. For milk and butter and cottage cheese we had our cow. There was Ima Dean's rooster which, in a pinch, could provide a meal and there was the pig. Still, when I considered the four mouths to be fed and the five months to be lived before the ground would thaw and the spring would again come our stores seemed not to be so abundant.

Our shelter itself was woeful, draftier than I

had ever noticed it to be before, each room now stacked along the wall with piles of cordwood higher than my head. The wood diminished the house and dirtied it. Traipsed by her pig, Devola was constantly sweeping. The pig was no problem; it shared a pallet with the rooster behind the kitchen stove. Three or four times a day Devola would take it outside to sniff and smell and run around. He didn't create any mess in the house.

But then there was the cow. Two days before Thanksgiving there came an unseasonable snow, just gently falling silver flakes at first but then turning into mean, stinging sleet and then a white fall so fast and thick that within the time of several hours the whole valley lay under a two-foot shawl of the stuff.

Romey feared for the cow's welfare and asked for a blanket. I told him there weren't any extra ones which was the truth and said anyway the warmth from the cow's body coupled with the cold would just probably create ice. I said, "This cow is hardy. Kiser said so. What does he do with his when it snows?"

"When he's home he herds them to their barn," replied Romey. "He's got a man taking care of them now. We need a barn for this cow. You want her to freeze to death?"

"Romey—"

"She won't take up much room. I'll fix her a nice bed right alongside mine with some nice straw."

"We don't have any nice straw, Romey, and besides—"

"Yes we do."

"Where'd we get it?"

"From Kiser's barn. Devola and Ima Dean took the wagon and went over there yesterday morning and got it. We got some nice cow food, too. Enough to last quite a while. Part of it's under my bed. You don't need to look at me like that, Mary Call Luther."

"Romey."

"What?"

"Nothing. Lord help us."

The cow was persuaded out of her pen and across the whitened yard and up the back steps which sagged under her weight but didn't break. In the kitchen the pig ran out from behind the stove and sniffed at her legs but the cow just looked at him and blinked. Romey prodded her to his room and the bed of straw. He said he was

worried about her toilet habits. What, he wondered, could be done about them.

I said I didn't know, that maybe the cow
could be trained as the pig had been.

"You could," murmured Ima Dean, "build her
a potty like the one I used to have."

"You crazy? How you gonna make a cow sit
on a potty?" said Romey. And the rest of us
laughed and his face flamed and he told us to
get out of his room and slammed the door hard
after us.

We ate fried cornmeal mush for supper and
drank hot milk. Before bedtime Romey took
the cow out for an airing. Devola and I wrapped
large, flat stones in pieces of wool flannel and
heated them in the oven and each of us carried
one of these to bed with us to tuck at the foot.

In the utter silence of that night some outside
sound woke me and I got up and looked out
across the frozen glitter and saw a gray fox sitting
on our fence, wild and tattered and hungry-
looking. In the morning it was gone. More snow
had fallen. Sugar Boy and Old Joshua appeared
softer and rounder against the eastering sky. All
of Trial Valley lay under a thick, sparkling com-
forter. Kiser's car had bonnets on it. Its wheels

were out of sight.

Romey said he was glad for the deep snow, that he'd rather study at home anyway and got out his books but just piddle-diddled over them. He milked the cow and fed her and led her out for a long, frigid airing. The static voice on the radio said to expect more snow and lower temperatures.

Devola and I went down to the root cellar and looked at our food supply. Devola said, "If we had a turkey I could roast him for our Thanksgiving dinner."

I said, "Yeah, if I had a crown I could be Queen of England, too. Here, take this squash. We'll have this and some nice pinto beans boiled up with a hunk of this nice salt pork instead. No, not two squashes, Devola. Just one. One's enough. We can cut it four ways."

Devola returned the extra squash to the bin, hovering her hand a little, yearning over this small loss but finally giving it up. In the brown gloom of the cellar her face was white, the fine, polished skin of it stretched smooth and lovely over the delicate bones. She cradled the one allowed squash in the crook of her sweatered arm. "It's stingy, just this one squash and beans for Thanksgiving dinner. When Roy Luther was alive we always had more."

I said, "Well, I can't argue with you about that because it's true. We glutted ourselves on Thanksgiving Day and went back to starving the day after. I remember how much fun that was. I wouldn't take a hundred dollars for the memory. Here. Take the other squash. Take two more. No? Changed your mind? Well why, for corn's sake?"

"You're mean, Mary Call."

"Sure, sure."

"And ugly."

"Sure, sure."

"You like being mean and ugly, don't you?"

"Of course. Being mean and ugly pleasures me more than anything I can think of. Opposite to what you think, I'm *glad* I'm not sweet and pretty like you. It takes time to be sweet and pretty and I haven't got any to spare. I'm too busy seeing to it that you and those other two up there don't starve to death and don't freeze to death and that the county people don't come and haul you away. How much of this pork do you want for tomorrow? You'd better tell me now; you won't get a second chance. When we go back upstairs I'm going to lock the door.

There's been some pilfering and it's got to stop."

Devola came to the table where the slabs of salt pork lay. She reached out and laid her hand on one of them, measuring a two-inch piece. "This much will be enough, I guess. I want to tell you something, Mary Call."

I cut off a three-inch piece. "I'm listening."

Hugging the squash, rubbing its dark green waxiness with her white fingers, Devola turned so that the mournful light, streaming down through the open door at the head of the steps, fell on her hair and across her shoulders. "I want to tell you I don't like how mean you are lately."

"You don't? I'm sorry."

"You think you're so smart, Mary Call Luther. You think you're funny, don't you?"

"Yeah. Look. I'm laughing. Ha, ha."

In a tender, remote voice Devola said, "You're not laughing. You're just being smart. But if you want me to I can tell you something that's funny. Yesterday before you and Romey got home from school there was a man here."

"A man? What man?"

"I don't know his name. He said Kiser sent him."

"What'd he want?"

"Nothing. He said where was Roy Luther and I told him asleep. Then we drank some tea."

"You drank some tea. How nice. And then what?"

"Then he said for me to put on my coat and go to town with him."

"What for?"

"I don't know. To see Kiser Pease in the hospital. He said Kiser wants to see me."

Well, I thought, I'm going to have to do something about Kiser, take some drastic steps of some kind. Even with two broken legs and a broken jaw he's not going to let up on us. One of these days he or somebody he sends will come hang-dogging it over here and this cloudy-headed one or one of the others will say something to really rile suspicion and then we'll be in it sure enough. Then there might be another grave have to be dug up on Old Joshua but as thin-lucked as I am I'd never get away with it. They'd hang me. Anyway I don't believe in killing. I'll have to think of something else. I wonder what it'd be like to be married to Kiser Pease. Maybe not so bad if I could get him to a dentist to get his teeth fixed up and get him to quit saying hit for it and ye for you. Mary Call

Luther Pease. Ugh.

I said, "Don't worry about what Kiser wants, Devola. He's no affair of ours. You did just right with this man yesterday, just right. Sure enough now, don't you want another squash for tomorrow? I was just joking you when I said only one."

"No," answered Devola. "This one will be enough. We'll make it be." And drifted toward the steps.

I put the cheesecloth and the protecting papers back over the salt pork slabs and we went back up the stairs to the kitchen. I locked the cellar door and put the key in my pocket. Romey had brought the radio to the kitchen; he and Ima Dean were huddled over it, fooling with its knobs. It had commenced to snow again. I heated a tub of water and Devola and I washed some wearing clothes and hung them on crisscrossed lines above the chairs and eating table. The sight of them, so thread-thin and gray, made me feel older than God.

That night part of our roof collapsed under the weight of the snow. Lying in the cold, still, one-o'clock darkness I heard it start—cracking and dropping and separating sounds, stealthy, so stealthy at first and paced, like the movements of a careful burglar. But then a beam crashed and then another and then there was a big, soft thud and I said to myself, That's no burglar, fool. That's this fool house falling down. The elements have finally caught up with it. And I got out of bed and lighted a lamp and put on my shoes and coat and went out and looked in the sitting room and saw Cosby Luther's rocker all splintered, lying on its side and snow on the floor and underneath it what had been the ceiling. I looked up and saw the night, only a reach or two away and nothing in between. It had turned off clear; the sky was peppered bright with stars.

Eventually I was able to get the rest of them out to share the adversity. They came and stood huddled and after a long, unstable moment said, "What happened?"

"Nothing," I answered. "I just thought the ceiling would look better lying on the floor than hanging up. What do you think? Come in and have a seat and tell me."

Romey lifted the skirt of his coat, which was an old one that had belonged to Roy Luther, stepped over two boards, shuffled through snow, stood looking down at Cosby Luther's rocker. "It's ruint."

"We might be able to fix it," I said. "But I don't know about the rest of this. I've just been sitting here wondering. Maybe the best thing to do would be just close the door and nail it shut and forget it till spring. What do you think?"

Romey knelt and put both his hands down on the fractured back of the rocker. His face silently convulsed. He stroked the rocker and the tears came to his eyes.

I said, "Well, we can't stay here the night like this. My guess is that the temperature's down to at least fifteen. I think the best thing to do is close this room off. What do the rest of you think?"

Yearning love and sympathy, Devola and Ima Dean went to Romey and leaned and awkwardly put their hands on his hair. They didn't speak; just patted his hair and made little soothing sounds. Trailed by the cocky bantam rooster, the pig appeared in the doorway and yawned.

I said, "Well, it's settled then. We'll just close this room off for the winter. We'd better salvage what furniture we can though. Can I get some help to do it or will I have to do it by myself?"

They ignored me. Ima Dean kissed the top of Romey's head and Devola patted his hand and said for him not to feel bad, that the rocker could be fixed. They raised him from it and lifted the chair and the three of them carried it out of the sitting room.

A sissy, I thought. My brother's turned into a real sissy, sniveling over a little thing like this. He's just like Roy Luther—no backbone. It'd serve them all right if I just sat here and froze to death. Then they'd *really* have something to beller about.

The pig had advanced into the room, was thirstily licking snow. The rooster ruffled his wings, hopped over to stand beside the pig, filled his throat with air, and foolishly crowed. A plop of snow fell on the bare calf of my leg and I looked up and saw the gray fox of the night before or one just like him. With his tattered back humped high and bristling and his eyes glowing red, he was crouched on the edge of the roof-hole hungrily looking down. His head was motionless, only his eyes moved, wary and mean, following the movements of the pig and the rooster.

Maybe I don't look like a human, I thought,

or maybe he's just so hungry he doesn't care about what I might do to him but in a minute he's going to jump. Lord, if You are present You'd sure better get word to me quick what to do and give me the strength to do it for right at this moment my bones are soup. Lord, don't let the rooster crow again; swelled up with air like that he looks twice as big as he really is. Lord, don't you think I'm in enough straits without this? If that fox was to land on me there's no question in my mind about who would come out best, and I honest haven't got the time to die or be sick even. Tell me what to do, Lord.

Something spoke to me and in the same instant that it did the rooster crowed and the fox jumped. I smelled it, its wild scent as it hurtled past me and landed almost on top of the pig. The pig screamed and the rooster squawked and flew straight up into the air and I saw my hand move, take up a splintered piece of two-by-four. The pig had slipped away from the fox, was teetering toward the door and the rooster had come down and was dancing in the snow; his terrorized shrieks rent the air.

The piece of two-by-four caught the fox square across the forehead. His eyes rolled up in his head. He reeled backward in the snow. I walked over to him and kicked him hard in the gut. He quivered once and was still.

Because I had to, I sat down again. I was a little sick to my stomach but I felt good. Not even a wild fox can lick me, I thought. I just proved it.

Romey and Ima Dean and Devola came back and said they'd put the rocker in Roy Luther's room. Then they spotted the fox and I had to tell them what had happened.

"It's a lesson," I said. "It's what it takes to get along in this world. Guts."

Ima Dean crept close and peered into my face. "You look very funny. Your eyes are very big."

"Help me up," I said to Romey and he put out his hand and grasped mine and it was then that I discovered the splinter in the soft, fleshy part of my hand, embedded deep, about a half inch wide and thick. Devola had to pull it out.

ELEVEN

THERE CAME A REVERSAL OF WINTER ALL in the passage of two or three days. The sun warmed and the winds quieted and turned spring-balmy. During the first part of this there were small floods, fed by the melting snow. The ground couldn't absorb the water fast enough, the floor of Trial Valley turned into a thick, brown ooze.

Devola turned our livestock and the rooster out, flung open all the doors and windows, gave Ima Dean a rag and a pail of soapy water, and they proceeded to scour everything in sight.

Romey put on his boots and I put on Roy Luther's and we went across the fields for a look at Trial Creek. Swollen to the top of its banks, clouded dark brown with silt, belching dirt and stones, and carrying blown branches along in its torrent, it had turned into an ugly, angered river.

In the near distance Sugar Boy and Old Joshua were shedding their snow mantles; their faces streamed with water.

I wondered how Roy Luther had made out in all of this but didn't speak my thought to Romey. Instead I said, "This won't last. I've seen false springs before. They always spell trouble. Next week there'll probably come the biggest blizzard in all history."

It was one of Romey's acquiescent days. He didn't even sigh when I said we shouldn't waste this time. He made the offer to go back to the house for our tools and the wagon, Mr. Connell's want list, and the wildcrafter's book.

In a sandy, wooded district, halfway up the side of Old Joshua, we harvested a worthwhile batch of princess pine, a small, creeping evergreen sometimes called ground holly, known by some as false wintergreen.

Going back down the mountain we passed close to Roy Luther's grave but didn't leave our path to go and look at it. Romey whistled a tune and said he wished he could have a picture of us—that it might give him a laugh someday if he did have, both of us with our hair wild and our clothes slung with mud, our boots so heavy with mud that we had to sit down and rid ourselves of it.

I said, "Yes, I'd like to have a picture of the way we look today, too. Then when I get to be the big shot that I aim to be someday and other big shots come into my office I'd show it to them."

"Your office," said Romey and laughed at this impossible dream.

This was the day Miss Goldie Pease, Kiser's sister, came sliding down the valley in her big, fine car, getting stuck in the slime and the ooze twice before reaching our front gate. She didn't resemble Kiser; she was squatter, with blue, waffled hair and a long humorless mouth. She stood on our topmost step and scraped mud from her shoes and said that at Kiser's request she had come all the way from southern Georgia to remove Kiser from the hospital and bring him home to do his convalescing. She said where was Roy Luther.

"He's asleep," I said.

She looked at me direct. "Asleep this time of day?"

"He's sick."

"What's the matter with him?"

"We don't know. He had a bad fall last summer. He doesn't rest at night anymore so I let him sleep all he can during the day. Was there something in particular you wanted to see him about?"

Miss Goldie Pease looked for a chair to sit on but there wasn't one; Devola had taken it inside. She regarded the fallen-down portion of our house. "There's some work over at Kiser's place needs to be done. I thought Roy Luther could do it. *This* place sure looks seedy. In fact, down-right disgraceful. Does Kiser know part of your roof has caved in?"

"No. It just happened a few days ago. It wouldn't differ to him if he did know though. He doesn't own this place anymore."

Miss Goldie Pease's eyes flew wide. "What do you mean he doesn't own this place anymore?"

"I mean he doesn't own it anymore. He signed it over to us months ago. This house and twenty acres of land. We don't work for him anymore. If Kiser's coming home he must be well. How's his jaw? Can he walk?"

A breeze made a futile attempt to ruffle the stiff, blue hair. Into the thick, unlovely face beneath it there came a slow, stirring look. "His

161

jaw's wired shut. He has a little trouble getting around. What do you mean he signed this place over to you months ago? Roy Luther pay him for it?"

"Not exactly; not in money. Kiser was terrible sick—maybe you don't know about that. But anyway he was and we went over and found him and saved his life. Then he signed a paper giving us this house and this land."

"Kiser's got a mighty short memory," said Goldie Pease. "This house and this land don't belong to Kiser; they belong to me. Clear over almost to where his barn sets, it all belongs to me. Let me see the paper he signed."

I showed her the paper and with a quick-curled lip she said it was worthless, that Roy Luther didn't have the sense to pound sand down a rat hole if he couldn't see how worthless it was. "I want to see him," she said. "Go wake him up and tell him to come out here. Him and me's got a few things to talk about."

Again I told her that Roy Luther was asleep and she looked at me and said, "Asleep. All right but when he wakes up tell him I'm over at Kiser's house. Tell him I want to see him. Tell him Kiser and me has had a little understanding about what is whose around here and it's come to Kiser's mind that this house and this land and the money it's been makin' belong to me and I mean to have it all back in my possession before the next forty-eight hours has passed."

She was mad and dead serious and she wasn't lying about the paper being worthless. I believed her when she said that when you give property away there's more to it than just signing a simple little paper agreement, that there are always legal details involved, that it has to be made a matter of public court records. Goldie Pease was not an educated woman but like a lot of people of her timber she was crafty. She wanted to look at the inside of the house and I took her in and showed her through it, all but Roy Luther's room. When we passed its closed door she just curled her lip. She said the place could be made livable, that she knew a couple down in Georgia who would just be tickled silly to live in it and farm her land and make money for her. She said that an end had come to Kiser's treasoning her.

The plight of the Luthers was none of her affair, she made that plain. We went back out on the porch and I said, "This trouble between you and Kiser. Well, you know it hasn't got anything

163

to do with us. Come spring Roy Luther'll be well enough to farm again. This is good land. He can make money from it for you."

"No," said Goldie Pease looking into the declining afternoon. "I don't want any of my brother's leftovers. I don't trust them. I want to start fresh. You tell Roy Luther I said I want you to vacate. Two weeks—that's what I'll give you to do it in. That's fair; it's the best I can do. Two weeks. You tell Roy I said that. You tell him I want to see him."

I followed her down the steps and out the gate to her car. "You going to bring Kiser home today?"

Goldie Pease got into her car and slammed the door. "No. I've changed my mind about that. I don't care if he never gets home. Him and his hoojer deals."

At the last minute of this visit she spotted Kiser's car and demanded the keys to it. I had to go back into the house and get them for her.

She only skidded once going back down the valley. I watched her do it and then right the car and go on.

Romey and Ima Dean and Devola, who had banished themselves during the visit, came around the corner of the house. Ima Dean said she had never seen anybody with blue hair before. With tender anxiety Devola asked where we were going to vacate to.

"I don't know yet," I said. "But just give me till tomorrow morning. I'll have it figured out by then."

Romey looked up at the sky which on the northern rim was beginning to fill with whorling, lead-colored clouds. So worried and agitated in his eyes but trying to hide his dismay and unease, he said maybe the weather would reprieve us from having to do anything right away, that the worst cold spell in the whole history of the state of North Carolina was moving down on us from the north according to the radio.

"Some reprieve," I said. "We'll probably all perish. That cussed Kiser Pease. He knew all along that paper was worthless when he signed it. Why didn't I know it? Because I'm ignorant, that's why. This is what comes of being ignorant. Ignorance always loses. I should have known I couldn't best that greasy outlaw."

"He's not a greasy outlaw," protested Devola. "I think he's nice. He's got the prettiest house."

"He's a greasy crook outlaw," I said, "and if you had the loyalty to me and Roy Luther that you're supposed to have you'd see that."

Romey said why was I bawling and I said I wasn't but I was. It scared them seeing me weaken like that and it scared me, too, because I knew we were in a bad fix, probably one of the worst we had ever been in and I didn't know what to do and there wasn't anybody to ask.

I started to take Roy Luther's shotgun and walk to town and find the hospital where Kiser was and the room he was in and walk in and blow his head off. I went so far as to take the gun down from the rack on the wall and put on my coat and start out but Romey came running after me. "You said yourself a gun never settled anything!" he shouted. "But if you didn't mean it, go ahead! Let 'em lock you up for being crazy, I don't care! We'll get along all right without you! The county people'll come and get us and take care of us! Go ahead! Go to town and find Kiser and blow his head off! He deserves it, I don't say he doesn't! But you just remember if you do, Mary Call Luther, I'll never believe another word you say!"

So then I had to go back inside with him and

put the gun away and try to think of another way. All during that loneliest and bleakest night I tried to think of a way out of our dilemma— where to find another roof for our heads and how to manage the move from the only home we had ever known to another without some- one's discovering that Roy Luther was gone from us. The new landlord, if we could find one, was bound to ask where our father was and if I said asleep . . . well, where do you hide a sleep- ing man during a trek from one place to another? If I said up in the mountains digging roots that would sound crazy. A ghost scamper- ing around the mountains digging roots in the dead of winter while his family waited for him to come down and arrange for a place for them to live. Crazy. Nobody wanted to rent a house to a ghost, least of all a crazy one. Anyway there weren't any houses to rent, not around Trial Valley.

I thought about a cave; maybe we could live in a cave.

The notion of all of us living in a hole in the side of a mountain and possibly freezing to death in it when winter settled down to do its worst didn't frighten me. Somehow it seemed a friendly idea, just for all of us to fall gently asleep in a cave some night and not ever wake up again—to be delivered from all the meanness and worry in life, forever safe.

The room in which I lay was very dark and by the minute turning colder. A strong wind had come up and was galing down the valley in great, bitter blasts. One of my brood made a sound in his sleep and I went from my bed for a look and after that, for the rest of that night, I didn't get warm again.

The false spring had gone. About five o'clock the next morning the storm slammed into us with all its blizzardous fury.

TWELVE

I T CLAMPED ITS ICY JAWS AROUND US AND
sucked us into its frigid mouth. The sky
opened and poured snow and the winds,
shrieking down from the mountain peaks, lifted
the white powder and drove it into drifts, some
of which I calculated to be as high as ten feet.
For three days the winds never let up.

Our water supply froze as did some of our
food in the root cellar though not the dried stuff
nor the pork. We melted snow and drank that
and cooked the vegetables and ate them anyway.
The beets were the worst. Our poor cow would
have frozen in her tracks had we not brought her
back inside the house. Romey had to give his
room entirely over to her; the smell that came
from it was not good and it was not now a
laughing matter.

Our electricity went off and stayed off and

now we were deprived of even the meager solace of the radio. Everybody grumbled and I said for them to be thankful for the wood-burning stove and the kerosene lamps.

I said to Romey that we should study and we lighted one of the lamps and spread our books on the kitchen table and had a lesson in geography but it was one of Romey's sullen days and one of my short-tempered ones so we didn't learn much about the beautiful, sun-burnished Bahama Islands.

Hating everything, most of all me, Romey said, "It wasn't like this when Roy Luther was alive. Why is that?"

"It was like this," I said. "It was just as bad. You just don't remember."

His thrust lip denied this. He fiddled with the lamp wick, turning it first high and then low. "Can Devola make us some fudge?"

"No."

"Why not?"

"Because we can't afford the sugar. Things may get worse."

Both with coats and head scarves on because the rest of the house was cold, Devola and Ima Dean left the warmth of the kitchen to go make beds. On the pallet behind the stove the pig snored and the rooster preened his feathers and hopped around searching for a forgotten morsel. Romey shuffled his books, with his hands explored the shape of his head and gazed at me out of eyes gaunt and bitter. "You're shore ugly."

"Yeah, well, some people are handsome and some are smart."

"I don't even think your hair's pretty anymore."

"I never said it was. I've just been taking your word for it all this time."

"You figured out where we're going to vacate to yet?"

"Not yet. I'm working on it though."

"What're you studying?"

"This price list Mr. Connell gave me. You see what it says here on the bottom? It says here that they're looking for new hands to make roping in their homes during the months of November and December. I wonder what kind of roping they mean."

"I don't know. I don't care. It's snowing harder. I wish it'd stop."

"It'll stop when the Lord wills it, not before."

Romey turned sideways in his chair, moved

his feet back and forth on the rung of it. He said, "The Lord has forgotten us. This land is forgotten. *We're* forgotten. We're forgotten people."

So harsh he said that but not with vigor. He said it like an old decayed man would say it—a truth filled with absolute despair. It was the most desolate, most disheartening thing I had ever heard anyone say and I didn't have any answer for it.

I looked at my brother and I thought, it's the truth. The Lord has forgotten us. This land is forgotten. We're forgotten people.

I thought about man's hold on life, how painful its struggle, and I tried to think of the reason for people like us Luthers ever having been born. There must be one, I thought. Roy Luther said there was a reason for everything. And something within me stirred and my spirits lifted and I thought, By the grace of the Lord we're here and what we make of it is our own affair. It's everybody's affair what they make of being here. The Lord hasn't forgotten us. Those are just Romey's words and he is just a child. This land isn't forgotten and neither are we. It just seems like we are out here in all the snow and cold and quiet.

There was a sudden break in the wind, it

ceased altogether just for a minute and in this I heard an audible silence. I thought about spring, how it would come again. How the mountains would turn fresh-green again and wave upon wave of returning warblers would come flashing across them wildly singing. The bluets and the trillium and lilies—all of the spring lovelies would bloom again. Spring would come—it always did.

My name is Mary Call Luther, I thought, and someday I'm going to be a big shot. I've got the guts to be one. I'm not going to let this beat me. If it does, everything else will for the rest of my life.

I said, "Romey, this is a bad time for us now but it's going to change. All we have to do is hang on. Your name is Luther, same as mine and that means you've got guts, same as me. Come on now; show them to me."

"You're crazy," muttered Romey and slammed the study books into a pile, scooped them up, and ran off to Roy Luther's room. I heard him yell to Devola that he didn't want his bed made, that he liked it wrinkled. The cow was mooing to be milked and I hollered for him to do it but he wouldn't; Devola had to.

An hour later we missed him; we looked everywhere but he was gone.

"I think I saw him put on his boots and his coat," tenderly offered Devola. "But then . . . well, he told me not to watch him so I didn't."

"Watch him do what?" I asked.

Devola hung her head. "He said he was going to town to see Kiser," she whispered. "He told me not to tell you."

So then I had to go after him.

At the back steps I sank in snow up to my waist. I struggled up out of it only to sink again. The wind bit into my face and the snowfall was so thick I was almost blinded with its whiteness. Though there was nothing but the blinding snow and the beating, suffocating wind I still screamed. "Romey! Romey!" hoping, somehow, to see him rise up out of the drifts.

Devola had opened the back door and was standing in its frame. She had Ima Dean by the hand and the wind was streaming their skirts straight out from their bodies and they were both crying and I shrieked to them to go back, go back, and Devola hesitated but then drew Ima Dean back inside and the door closed and again there was just the blizzard and me out there. I floundered to the corner of the house and went around it and cupped my hands over my eyes and peered out over the grim, glittering snowscape. The fence had sunk completely out of sight. Beyond where I knew it to be the fields stretched empty, not one moving speck on them. There was only the wind and the snow.

I floundered to the fence and found the gate and tried to push it open, for what reason I don't know for at a time like that what difference does it make whether you walk through a gate or just lift your legs and flop over? I lifted my legs and flopped over and fell face down in a deep pile of cold, wet snow. It closed over me and for a minute I just lay there gasping and I think bawling and with a rushing blackness inside my head. But then the blackness cleared and I said to myself, Well, come on, Guts Luther. You're the one always carping about guts. Let's see yours now. And I pushed myself up and hobbled out to where I knew the road to be and started down the valley bawling, "Romey! Romey!" every foot of the way.

Halfway down the valley I found him lying asprawl in a drift, near frozen. He didn't want to get up but I made him. He said he couldn't walk, that there was something wrong with one of his ankles.

I said, "That's too bad. I don't feel so good myself. But you're going to get up and you're going to walk home, Romey Luther. I'm not about to carry you."

His ankle was badly sprained. Devola had to cut his rubber boot off. I said, "While you're at it cut his throat, too. We could have been killed out there. A blizzard is nothing to fool around with. I should like to know what you thought you were doing."

Romey gritted his teeth as Devola pulled the slaughtered boot from his leg. He said, "I was goin' to town to see Kiser."

"What for, for corn's sake?"

"To get him to pay his sister for his house and property so's we could stay on here. To get him to make good the paper he signed."

"You think you could do that, huh? You think you could get him to change just like that, huh?"

Romey glanced at Devola and then Ima Dean and then looked at me. To hide the tears he lowered his eyes. "I was going to beg him," he whispered. "I thought if I begged him he'd make things right."

"Beg Kiser Pease," I said. "Better we all go live in a hole in the ground. We're not going to beg Kiser Pease for anything, Romey. We're not going to beg anything from anybody. Charity is one of the worst things there is. It does terrible things to people."

The tears slipped down and were angrily brushed away. "What things?"

"It demeans people."

"What's that mean?"

"When you demean somebody you make them smaller than they are. You conquer them and then they have to be humble and toady to you. For this to happen to us—for us to humble ourselves and toady to anybody—is one of the things I promised Roy Luther never to let happen. On my highest word of honor I promised him that and I mean to keep the promise so you can just forget about begging Kiser Pease or anybody else for anything. If you sneak off again to try it and I have to go after you and bring you back I'll lock you in the root cellar and put you on bread and water for a week."

Devola had applied snow to Romey's ankle until he howled with how cold it was. Now she was tearing strips from an old, soft sheet to bind it. With deft fingers she scooped homemade slippery elm salve from a jar, gently smoothing it on the swelling, took the strips and wound them round and round tight. Watching her I thought, she should be a doctor. Or a nurse. There is so much more to her than people realize. Roy Luther never realized how much there is to her and I, myself, am guilty of this, too. And all of it is going to slip by and be wasted unless I can think of a better way for her.

O Lord, help me to think of a better way for all of us.

Outside a new sound had begun—rain. It rained all the rest of that day and all that night, eroding the snow, dissipating the wind-formed ridges of it, sheathing the bare branches and all of the valley in gleaming, brittle ice.

At the window with his crippled foot propped on a pillow, Romey reported smoke coming from the chimney of Kiser's house. He didn't say it but I knew he was thinking it the same as I: How short our time had grown, consumed by the blizzard and the rain and how still there wasn't the sign of any answer for us in sight. We had had our reprieve but now it was close to an end. Goldie Pease wasn't the kind to commute a sentence. She'd bodily set us out in the fields when the time came and then she'd see that Roy Luther wasn't with us and then she'd go flying into town and blab to the county people and then they'd come and separate us and then . . .

Backward and forward and up and down, my mind had shuttled over the problem a million times and I couldn't see any answer for it but one: I would marry Kiser Pease myself. Fourteen years or no I'd do it. Kiser was simple—he could be persuaded. And right after the ceremony, performed in whatever place by whatever outlaw, I'd assert myself to my wife's rights. I'd make Kiser pay Goldie Pease off for the Luther house and land and put the deed in Devola's name. And then, right after that was done, I'd bid Kiser farewell. Then in the peace God intended for us all we Luthers would live in our part of the valley and Kiser could live in his if he so chose. If he did so choose I'd plant a row of dense trees between his place and ours so that I'd never have to look at him again, nor even his smoke coming up out of his chimney with the witch's keyhole near the top.

THIRTEEN

JUST AT DAYLIGHT THE NEXT MORNING I started out on my mission, leaving a note behind to tell my brood merely that I had gone to see about a new place for us to live and to not let Goldie Pease, if she came, past the threshold.

The valley lay encrusted in an iced calm, the road now blown clean of snow, with troughs of ice in its frozen ruts. The sun was appearing; against the slowly coloring sky Old Joshua and Sugar Boy shone harshly pure.

There were remote noises: branches breaking, cracking sharply beneath the weight of ice. But all life had flown. Taking a shortcut to the main road I saw a dead hare lying on its side on a pillow of soiled snow.

The rain and snow plows had cleared the county road. It wasn't so bad walking. Had I not such a worry on my mind I would have enjoyed the trip.

About halfway to town Mr. Connell pulled up alongside in his truck and told me to climb in and ride. He said he was on his way to the abattoir on the other side of town; said where was I going and I said to the hospital to see Kiser Pease about a little pressing business. He said how had we made out during the blizzard and I said fine. He asked how Roy Luther was and I said fine. He said how about me being his breakfast guest and pulled up in front of a roadside cafe and we went in and ate fried eggs and country ham and sugared doughnuts.

This town I speak of was of no importance to me, the store windows all dressed in displays of finery beyond the Luther reach: soft leather boots with fur cuffs, dresses trimmed in lace and winking glass buttons, flared coats and straight ones, one of these with a red, cowled hood and a wisp of throat-scarf, jeweled in its center.

The window of the drugstore was dim but inside I could see a white-coated man moving about and I wondered what medicine he was concocting from what roots and herbs.

In one block I counted three churches and I

said to Mr. Connell that the townspeople must be uncommonly good. He said, "They ain't. They're just runnin' scared like everybody else."

He was kind enough to let me out at the door of the hospital. "How you going to get back?" he asked.

I said, "Shanks' mare," borrowing an expression of Roy Luther's and Mr. Connell laughed and drove off.

Only in my imagination had I ever been inside a hospital. I had always imagined them to be places of brisk activity; doctors tearing in and out of rooms barking life-saving orders and nurses leaping around carrying them out. I had always thought the inside of a hospital would be rustling with energy and motion, and would be light and bright.

This one was none of those things. There was an old man in a coat-sweater who was mopping the entrance room with a dirty mop but no nurses or doctors. There was a sign on the desk which said RING BELL and I went up to it and rang it but nobody came. I then asked the mopper where was Kiser Pease's room and he shifted the liquid wad bulging in his lower lip and said he didn't know, that the desk nurse would be back soon, for me to sit down and wait.

I sat down and waited. I breathed the melancholy air and looked at the dingy walls. The old man slopped syrupy water from his wooden bucket, went off someplace to spit, returned wiping his mouth on his sleeve, flopped his dirty mop, and took not the slightest interest in me. Presently he shuffled off.

From the corridors which opened out to the left of this room and to the right of it there came the tintinnabulation that goes with a meal—dishes and eating-ware clanking. And after a bit of listening to this and watching the clock on the wall, the hands sweeping around and round, I chose one of the corridors to investigate and walked down its dim, linoleumed way, nobody stopping me. I pushed on a door and went in it several steps and realized that I was in a place where operations were done. There were two doctors and two nurses and a patient on a table. I couldn't see the patient though; he was receiving too much attention. Nobody looked up at me. I got out of there quick.

After that I found Kiser's room. With the aid of crutches he was hobbling up and down and back and forth. He seemed uncommonly glad to see me. He couldn't move his jaw; to allow the broken bones in it to grow together again it was wired shut but he was able to talk to me through clenched teeth. He asked had I come with Goldie? He shambled to the door and opened it and looked out, expecting, I think, to see her standing there. I said, "Kiser, I came by myself. Is it all right if I sit in this chair?"

He slammed the door and hobbled back to sit on the side of his bed. "This is the closest I ever come to bein' in jail," he said. "How ye be, Mary Call?"

"Oh, I'm peart as a cricket, Kiser. My, you've turned thin. But it's kind of becoming."

Kiser turned a tragic gaze. "I can't eat. Have to suck my meals through a straw. I'm sick and nobody cares. You seen my sister?"

"Your sister? Oh, sure. She's living in your house. You want a drink of water or anything, Kiser? You're so pale. Maybe you'd better lie down."

Kiser's smile was wan. "I don't want to lie down. I've *been* lyin' down. I'm sick and nobody cares. My sister was supposed to've come after me days ago and take me home. Until I'm better

I can't fend for myself."

"No, you don't look like you're in any position to do that, Kiser. It's bad out in the valley right now. There's about three feet of mud and no electric power—at least not at our place. Why don't you phone your sister and remind her she's supposed to come after you and take you home? Maybe she's forgotten."

Kiser punched the foot rail of his bed with one of his crutches. "Don't have a phone in my house. Anyway, I've changed my mind about wantin' Goldie to do anything for me. How's Devola?"

"Oh, she's fine."

"The cow givin' you plenty of milk?"

"Oh, sure."

"How's the pig?"

"He's fine?"

"You'uns haven't slaughtered him yet?"

"No."

"How's Roy Luther?"

"He's fine."

"Is he still queer in the head?"

"A little. He's getting better though. I reckon by spring he'll be all recovered."

With his strong hands Kiser raised both of his

crutches up straight into the air and clacked them together. "I sure would like to get out of this place and go home but I got nobody to take care of me until I get well enough to do it myself. Goldie . . . well, Goldie, I'm a-thinkin' she's mad at me for some piddle-diddle thing. She's always been touchy. If she ain't going to do what I asked her to come up here and do I wish she'd get out of my house and go on back to Georgia. She ain't doin' me one bit of good, sittin' out there in my house, pawin' through all my personal stuff and eatin' up my vittles. You say you'd seen her, Mary Call?"

"Yeah. She stopped by one day just before the blizzard."

"What'd she have to say?"

"I dunno. She and Roy Luther talked some."

"What about?"

"I dunno. I'm not a door-crack listener, Kiser."

"I suppose she told him how crooked I am and how much I've beat her out of. Goldie was always a good hand at packin' her own wrong-doin's off on to other people."

"Is that so?"

Kiser clacked his crutches again. "Yes, that's

so. She's been doin' it all her life. And of course her bein' a woman everybody thinks she's weak and can't help herself so they take her side against me."

"She didn't look weak to me," I said. "I didn't take sides with her against you. I'm sure Roy Luther didn't either."

Kiser stood the crutches upright on the floor. He swung his mending legs. He raised the crutches and laid them flat across the foot of the bed. The collar of the hospital robe gaped open to show me his striped pajamas underneath. They looked clean enough but Kiser was embarrassed. He put his hand up to the collar and held it there. With a doleful and afflicted look he said, "I sure need to get out of here. This place is killin' my nerves. But I got nobody to watch out for me till I get well again. Goldie, she ain't goin' to do nuthin' for me. I can see that now. And after I paid her way up here, too. I sent her forty dollars."

I thought the moment was right. "Kiser," I said, "how would you like to get married?"

Kiser's dangled legs jerked. He sucked his breath in sharp. He inched himself slowly backward on the bed and the crutches at the foot of it shifted and slid off and clattered to the floor. I made a move to rise and pick them up but Kiser, with a flurried movement of his hand, said for me to let them be. He said, "What was that you said just now, Mary Call? I don't think I heard you right."

"Kiser," I said again. "How would you like to get married?"

Eagerness and caution tracked across Kiser's lean face in two swift, opposite tides. His legs jerked again. He stared at me. "I'd like it. I'll be good to her. I'll be good to all of you'uns. You-all can come have dinner with Devola and me every Sunday. When can it happen?"

"Kiser—"

"I'll give you another pig. Maybe two. And I'll fix the roof to your place. Last time I was over there I noticed it was in pretty bad shape. And I'll buy you a refrigerator. A great big one. I bin meanin' to do that anyways. Ain't no sense in anybody bein' without a refrigerator this day and time."

"Kiser—"

"And I'll give Roy Luther some land. Ain't no sense in a man bein' as hoggish about his land as I've been. He should share what he don't need.

Law, there's aplenty of it. Eh, law! I reckon there is! I must own at least a thousand acres. That's a heap of land. One man don't need it all. Even if he was to have a son or two one man don't need it all. There's aplenty for everybody. Devola and me'll only need . . . well, off hand I can't say how much we'll need. That'll depend. But we won't need it all. You tell Roy Luther I aim to give him some land. You tell him I said—"

"Kiser."

"What? Well, what?"

"Kiser," I said. "I'm not talking about you marrying Devola. You know I can't let that happen. Not ever. I promised Roy Luther that and I mean to keep my promise. What I'm talking about is . . . well, I thought you might like to marry *me*."

"You!"

"Yes. I know there's a lot of difference in our ages and all. You're most forty and I'm—"

"Most forty! *I'm* most forty? Who said so?"

"I don't know. Somebody. I just thought . . . Kiser, I don't care how old you are. I love you and I want to marry you."

"I'm thirty," said Kiser.

"All right, you're thirty then. I don't care. It

doesn't make any difference. But I love you and want to marry you."

"*You* love *me?*"

"I might. Yes, I do. I love you."

"And you want to *marry* me?"

"I didn't say I *wanted* to . . . well, yes. That's right. I want to marry you. How about it?"

Kiser pinched his nose and violently pulled on both ears. He tightened the sash on his robe. He looked at the tasseled end of it and slowly, with great absorption, extracted two long silken threads from it. They didn't want to come loose but he pulled at them until they did. He said, "Aw, Mary Call."

"What?"

"You don't love me."

"Yes, I do. How do you know I don't? Listen, Kiser, when somebody tells you they love you you're not supposed to—"

"You don't love me. You got no more use for me than you've got for a clod of dirt."

"Why, that's not true! I have so got use for you! I've got so much use for you that . . . listen, Kiser, you're making me mad now! I didn't come all the way from Trial Valley just to sit here and be insulted!"

"Mary Call, I haven't insulted you."

"Why, you have so! You've as much as called me a liar! Listen, Kiser, do you want to marry me or don't you?"

"No," answered Kiser and hung his head.

"You rotten, stinking . . . you old . . . you treasoner you! You think I don't know how you've treasoned us? Signing that worthless piece of paper? Your sister owns the land you gave us for saving your worthless life! And the house we're in, too! She told me you were supposed to have paid her for it years ago but never did! And now she wants it back! So now we've got to vacate it! You've treasoned me the same way you did Roy Luther! You treasoned him to his grave! Ohhhhhhh! If I had the sense I was born with I'd have brought his shotgun and blown your worthless head off!"

"Mary Call—"

"Oh, shut up. You make me sick to my stomach. Your rotten teeth and your witch's keyhole. You're right about one thing. I've got no more use for you than I have for a clod of dirt. Not as much!"

"Wal, it's nothin' to bawl about," said Kiser.

"Who's bawling? You ever see me bawl?

When you do, put it in the newspaper for every-body to read, it'll be that unusual. Here are your crutches. Oops! I didn't mean to bang you like that. Did it hurt?"

"No," replied Kiser, rubbing his banged fore-head. "Mary Call, wait a minute. Now just wait a minute."

I didn't want to hear what else he had to say. I had demeaned myself to him, that was the part that hurt, not the other. I think I bawled all the way home.

They wanted to know where we were going to live and I said, "In a cave and don't think we're the first ones who ever did it. People have been living in caves since the beginning of time. And enjoying it, too. We'll be troglodytes. Isn't that an interesting word? Troglodyte?"

"Yes," agreed Romey. "But I don't see . . . *what* cave are we going to live in, Mary Call?"

"Oh, I don't know that yet. I have to go and find one. I'll go in just a minute, just as soon as I catch my breath. Don't worry, I'll find one. I'll find a good one and we'll fix it up real livable. We'll get some heavy paper from Mr. Connell and we'll paper the walls and if we can't get this linoleum up to take with us we'll buy some new. We've got money in the money box. Don't worry, we'll be real snug and cozy."

"Will we still go to school?" inquired Romey.

"Of course. Being a troglodyte doesn't excuse you from having to learn. Oh, I *wish* we had another wagon. I can just see us having to make about a hundred trips back and forth with just the one. We'll need some boxes to pack stuff in. Do we have any boxes?"

Devola went to the root cellar and returned with two cardboard boxes. Tenderly opposing, she said, "Mary Call, we can't live in a cave. Can we?"

"Sure we can. What's to stop us? Don't worry. I've got it all figured out. I'll find one with two parts to it if possible. We'll sleep in the back part and live in the front. We'll take this stove apart and take it up first. We'll need it to heat with and cook on. I don't know if we'll take all these chairs. We may not have room for them. But we'll take this table and Cosby Luther's rocker and her chest—we won't leave those behind. And of course we'll take our beds."

Ima Dean was worried about the bathroom. She said what would we do about that part and

I said we'd have to make one. Nobody asked what we would do about electricity; they knew we'd just have to do without it for a while. All three were so good not to voice all the obstacles we would surely encounter. Romey said when spring came we could start building a house, couldn't we?

I said, "Yes, when spring comes we'll start making money again with our roots and herbs. We'll make lots of it because that's the best time for root 'n' herbers. Then we'll be able to afford all the lumber we need and we'll build ourselves a nice house. We'll have a yellow kitchen and hot water."

By that time it was middle afternoon. The sun was valiantly shining and the air had warmed. Trial Valley lay in the clear, yellow color of this winter warmth but as I left its floor and started the ascent up the slopes of Old Joshua the warmth diminished. A cloud drift descended and the air turned wet and cold. I went up and up, leaving my trailway at one point to seek out Roy Luther's grave and to stand beside it for one sober moment. I tried to feel his presence but felt nothing. I heard the silence, so still. A mound of smooth, white snow lay upon his grave and I looked down upon it and tried to think that we were having some kind of communion with each other but found that a curious thing had happened: I could only dimly remember at all the sound of his voice. I felt a sense of betrayal but then I thought, Oh, for corn's sake. Even if he could speak to you he couldn't tell you what to do, fool.

So then I went on and found the cave I thought we could live in, a black hole in the cheek of Old Joshua. Striking matches, using up a whole box of them, I explored its deepest interior. It was icy cold and very dark but was large and had an even floor and I said to myself, It will do. It will *have* to do. We'll *make* it do. It won't be for long; just until the spring. When spring comes we'll build a house. And I went home to tell them.

Kiser Pease was there, sitting at the table in the kitchen like he owned it. Devola was sitting opposite him with her hands folded and her face quiet. Romey and Ima Dean were playing jacks in a corner of the room.

I said to Kiser, "Well, I see you made it back to Trial Valley under your own power."

"I took a taxi out from town," he said.

"Devola and me've been sittin' here talking, Mary Call."

"Yeah? About what?"

Devola had put her hair up and now, whether by some trick of the light or maybe it was real, she looked as I remembered Cosby Luther to look in the time of a family crisis, deep and strong with a kind of grand, maternal dignity. She told me to take my coat and boots off and come sit down with her and Kiser and I obeyed her as I would have Cosby Luther. Firmer than I had ever heard her speak she said, "Mary Call, Kiser has paid his sister for this house and the twenty acres of land he gave us the night we saved his life so that part's all straight now."

"It's straight," said Kiser. "I paid my sister and tomorrow I'll go to the courthouse and fix up the deed in Devola's name. I'd put it in yours, Mary Call, but you're still a minor."

"Kiser and I are going to get married," said Devola in still a firmer voice. "Don't look so tough, Mary Call. It makes you ugly."

I was tired, so tired. I didn't feel tough; all I felt was an immense weariness. "Married," I said. "No, you can't do that. I promised Roy Luther never to let that happen. I've found us a place to live in, Devola. Tomorrow we're going to start moving. What about supper? Are we going to have any?"

"Seems to me," remarked Kiser in an offhand way, "like Roy Luther put a lot off on to you that didn't belong."

"He didn't," I said. "He didn't put anything off on to me that didn't belong. He knew I was tough and strong and he knew I could do everything he ordered. What about supper, Devola?"

"She looks sick," Kiser said to Devola.

I heard him say that and I saw him stand. She stood, too, and I saw their faces wavering, hovering, kind anxiety in them, and love, too. What funny looks, I thought. How sickening, to let their feelings show like that.

"I'll make her some tea and put her to bed," I heard Devola say to Kiser.

I said, "Don't want any tea and don't want bed. You aren't going to marry Kiser; I promised Roy Luther never to let that happen and I mean to keep my promise. We're going to move tomorrow; going to live in a cave. Be troglodytes. I've got it all figured out. Roy Luther is dead, Devola. Oh, he's dead. Oh, oh."

"Shhhhhhhh," said Devola. "It's all right. You

did the best you could. You did real good. But now you've got to let us help you."

"Never mind the tea," said Kiser. "Let's just get her to bed."

"I don't want bed," I said, and stood up and fainted.

FOURTEEN

S O THEN THERE CAME THIS TIME OF MY
having to say to Romey that Roy Luther
and I had erred a little in our judgment of
Devola. "Of course Roy Luther didn't know she
was going to change," I said. "That's why he
made me make him the promise I did. But you
see her now. You see how she's changed. If I went
to a judge now and told him she was cloudy-
headed he'd think I was. Bring me the money
box, Romey."

Romey shot me an alarmed look. "What
for?"

"I want to see how much money is in it."

"There's as much in it as the last time we
looked," said Romey. "Lookit my ankle. See? It'll
all well again. What'd Miss Breathitt want? You
didn't tell me."

"She wanted to know when we were coming

back to school."

"What'd you tell her?"

"I told her we'd probably be there Monday. About the money, Romey—"

Desperately Romey explored the shape of his head with his hands. "No. I say no. I know what you want to count it for and I say no. If Devola needs a new dress and new shoes to get married in I say let Kiser buy 'em for her. He's got lots of money."

"Romey," I said, "we're Luthers. Are you forgetting what that means?"

"No. How could I? You remind me every day. But I just don't see why *we* have to buy her wedding stuff. Kiser's the one wants to marry her. If he wants her to look nice for their wedding let *him* buy her clothes. He said he would. I heard him."

"Romey."

"Oh, rats," said Romey but without any more arguing climbed up and got the money box.

I would have preferred Devola to get married in her own home but we couldn't manage it— couldn't get our sitting room restored to normal in time. So on a Sunday afternoon at two o'clock all of us gathered in Kiser's parlor to listen to the preacher perform the union, Kiser in a new gray suit and Devola in a new yellow dress and yellow shoes.

The preacher had brought along a violin and a lady to play it. Kiser's jaw was healed—he didn't have to speak clenched through his teeth anymore but did anyway. When the preacher asked, do you, Kiser Pease, take this woman to be your lawful wedded wife, Kiser's face went blind and turned sheer white but Devola turned her head and smiled at him and he recovered. Then the preacher asked Devola if she took Kiser to be her lawful wedded husband and she said she did and then the violin lady soared a piece and then we ate three-layered cake and peppermint ice cream and drank coffee.

Romey went outside to look at something and came back and whispered to me that Kiser's witch's keyhole was gone—that it had been cemented over.

Devola wrapped three slices of the cake and gave them to Ima Dean to take home. Kiser persuaded me down to his basement and tried to force a ham and a wad of money on me, got mad at me when I wouldn't take either. "You don't need to get that stubborn look on you, Mary

Call. I'm your brother-in-law now whether you like it or not and I guess I got a right to help you if I want."

I said, "Kiser, you didn't marry *all* of the Luthers. Just Devola. Best we get that straight today."

Kiser flapped his arms in silent frustration.

"Just you be good to Devola," I said. "The rest of us will make out all right. We're making Christmas roping now and come spring we'll be out again with our roots and herbs."

"Roots 'n' herbs," said Kiser and turned a lonely look. "You'uns are a-goin' to kill yourselves stumblin' around up there on those mountains. It ain't right."

"It's right," I said. "It's the rightest thing that ever happened to us."

"I'm kind of guardian to you and Romey and Ima Dean now," said Kiser. "I got that fixed up with the county people. So you got to halfways listen to what I say, Mary Call."

"Okay, Kiser, but just don't go borrowing any trouble. I won't give you any trouble if you don't give me any."

"Goin' to build you a barn," said Kiser. "Right away. So's you can move those animals out of your house. You hear me, Mary Call?"

"Yeah, Kiser. Sure. That's nice."

At first it was strange without Devola. For one thing I now had to do all the cooking and cleaning and then there was the problem of Ima Dean. She howled when I said she couldn't go to school with me, balked at having to stay with Devola on school days. She said it was lonesome at Devola's house. "Why can't I go to school and be in the first grade and learn how to read?" she asked.

"Because you're too young," I answered. "Go color a picture or cut out some paper dolls. I'm trying to study and you're bothering me."

"I have *got* to learn how to read," said Ima Dean. "If you loved me you'd teach me. If I knew how to read I wouldn't be lonesome when you're gone to school."

So then I had to teach her how to read and this and the roping, done at night and on Saturdays and Sundays, sped the winter by.

At making roping, which you see towns decorated with at Christmastime, Romey was more adept than I. He could sit at the little hand-driven machine and crank out fifty yards of it in less than two hours. With one hand he'd lift the hemlock or balsam or white pine tips which we had gathered earlier and place them, one at a time, on the stout twine with which the machine was threaded. Two turns of the crank and wire, fed from a spool beneath the twine, fastened the green tips securely, wire and twine twisted, hidden within the crisp greenery.

It was Mr. Connell who got us the machine. In his car he took us into town to the drug company which sold the roping—shipping it everywhere at Christmastime—and explained to the man there that we needed to make money and gave him the cash to lease the machine out of his own pocket. We received an hour's instruction, bought some spools of wire and some balls of twine, went home and, after harvesting ten gunnysacks of white pine, balsam, and hemlock tips, started to work.

The house filled with the scent of the rich, fragrant green stuff. Behind the stove the pig, given to us by Devola, snored on his pallet, the rooster beside him. Ima Dean sat at the open oven door, toasting herself and reading. Romey and I took turns at the machine. It snowed. But even this was pleasant. The hardest of our worries were gone.

I had asked Mr. Connell how his wife felt about us now everybody knew Roy Luther was dead and his answer had been that if I was doing any worrying about Mrs. Connell I was wasting my time.

There was an evening when Kiser came and said, "I got the business of Roy Luther straightened out today, Mary Call. He can be left where he is, up on Old Joshua."

"It's where he wanted to be," I said. "Thank you."

"You're welcome," said Kiser and grinned wide and I saw then his newly repaired teeth, shining white and clean and perfect.

It would have been wrong to take notice of them in words so I didn't.

FIFTEEN

SPRING IS A WONDROUS NECESSITY. I thought it would never come. I thought the hoary winter would never leave us. At night, after the others had gone to bed, I would go outside and stand in the snow and look out across the hard, white fields and think, *This* year it won't come. Only a miracle could bring it. It's such an old story, spring. Surely the earth must be tired of having to produce it year after year. These mountains are reckoned to be two billion, five hundred million years old. Surely the earth must be tired of supporting them. Spring won't come again. How can it? Everything is so frozen. Romey was right; this is forgotten land. The Lord has forgotten us. We are forgotten people.

Shivering, not so much with the cold as with my thoughts, I would walk around the house and out to the gate and stand leaning against it and look up at Sugar Boy and Old Joshua. And I would think, They're never going to be green again. It had to come to an end sometime. This is probably the year for it.

Such childish thoughts those were and wasted ones. For the spring came as it always did, silently unfolding, pushing, pulling, budding, splitting.

Flushed with this rebirth Trial Valley turned tender green. The air softened and the warblers came, a great, showy wave of them, flashing down into the valley, singing, darting, flitting from tree to bush and back again, all so curious and alive and glad to be home.

The juncos came out of their hiding places in the woods and perched on our fence and trilled their sweet bell-songs. All of the birds came back; the flickers, the robins, the goldfinches, all of them.

Before the trees put on full leaf the wild flowers bloomed: bloodroot, lady slippers, trillium, trout lilies, fawn lilies, and the dainty, nodding lilies-of-the-valley. The "sarvice" trees—correctly known to some as shadbush or service trees—flowered downy-white on the slopes of Old Joshua and Sugar Boy.

This was spring in Trial Valley, the season of the bountiful bud.

On a Saturday morning Romey, Ima Dean, and I went across the fields to Trial Creek and followed it up to where the balm of Gilead trees grew sixty to one hundred feet high. Ima Dean held our basket and Romey and I hooked the branches with our rakes, pulling them down, to reach the oblong, waxy buds. The oozing wax from them turned our fingers sticky and yellow. The sun was in our eyes and in our mouths. We went from tree to tree and filled the basket. In the way of mountain people Romey and Ima Dean persisted in calling the buds "bammy Gillet." They wouldn't heed my correction, just laughed at it and said how stuck up I was.

We talked about the days to come, how busy we would be with our harvesting. Across the creek in a marshy hollow there was a patch of skunk cabbage, green and shiny, its ovate leaves already a foot high. The roots and rootsticks of these plants were worth money. On another day we would be back for them. And yet on another we would follow the stream down to where the graceful black willows grew. The fluffy catkins of these yield pollen.

In the days to come we would gather blue pimpernel, wild indigo, mayapple, maypop, sweet elder, horse nettle berries, catnip and sassafras leaves. We would go out with our wagon and our book and our digging and cutting tools and bring home boneset herbs and red clover flowers. We would dig for hellebore, hydrangea, butterfly, and blue cohosh roots. We would gather log moss and dry it. We would harvest sumac and black haw and fringe tree bark. There was so much of this we would do and so many different names I cannot tell them all here. The mountains and valleys of North Carolina are rich in these wild medicine plants. We discovered them and it was a fine education.

The Cleavers write about
WHERE THE LILIES BLOOM

"In this work we have explored 'wildcrafting,' the harvesting of wild buds, roots, leaves and bark. Throughout Western North Carolina and reportedly throughout all of the Appalachian region there are whole families who occupy themselves thus and earn a fair living at it, but this is not an occupation for the lazy, the squeamish or the fainthearted.

"When we first went to Boone, N.C., and established a home there we were uncommonly impressed with the friendliness and the simplicity and the genuineness of the people. . . . They envy no one. The real mountaineer is proud and independent. . . . On a mountain road, way back in a thick forest, we saw an old woman and her grandson gathering pollen and picking leaves. Curiosity led us to stop and ask questions, and we found a new friend and the idea for *Where the Lilies Bloom*. Later on we went through the huge botanical warehouse in Boone—the Wilcox Drug Company—and saw the mountain people coming in with their precious harvests. They talked with us freely and invited us to their homes and we went, and *Where the Lilies Bloom* began to take on definite, exciting shape. All of the names and incidents in the book are fictitious of course. Writing the book was pure pleasure."